J. P. Baker

The Tide Over the Horizon

Bumblebee Books
London

BUMBLEBEE PAPERBACK EDITION

Copyright © J. P. Baker 2023

The right of J. P. Baker to be identified as author of this work has been asserted in accordance with sections 77 and 78 of the Copyright, Designs and Patents Act 1988.

All Rights Reserved

No reproduction, copy or transmission of this publication may be made without written permission.
No paragraph of this publication may be reproduced, copied or transmitted save with the written permission of the publisher, or in accordance with the provisions of the Copyright Act 1956 (as amended).

Any person who commits any unauthorised act in relation to this publication may be liable to criminal prosecution and civil claims for damage.

A CIP catalogue record for this title is available from the British Library.

ISBN: 978-1-83934-725-2

Bumblebee Books is an imprint of
Olympia Publishers.

First Published in 2023

Bumblebee Books
Tallis House
2 Tallis Street
London
EC4Y 0AB

Printed in Great Britain
www.olympiapublishers.com

Chapter 1
Beneath the Waves

Tetra was getting tired of living on an island with nothing to do. She dreamed of adventure; from cascading down the pyramids to climbing above Mount Everest. There was so much in the world to see and do that Tetra often thought of herself as trapped in a fish tank, swimming endlessly around the same place without any hope of escaping. There was a journey to be had somewhere, if only someone or something could pull the plug on the sea, so she could watch the ocean drain away and then make her escape.

"There's nothing to do on this island!" Tetra would often scream in frustration.

"Some people would call this island paradise," her mum would often reply.

"Those people haven't had to walk in circles their whole lives," Tetra would retort.

It wasn't that the island was uniquely boring or uniquely blissful, but rather it was uniquely static. The same market with the same shops, the same familiar faces with the same jobs, even the wind blew the same way, without the imagination to take a different route. The island had beautiful, golden beaches that surrounded a tiny jungle in the middle, that leaned against the steep slope of a small mountain. Just like its people, it had been this way for many centuries.

Today, like many days before it, was one filled with a blue sky and a glaring sun. The day was still young, but time had a habit of moving quicker when Tetra least wanted it to. Indeed, a day of procrastinating by the docks could easily become two days if they weren't broken up by the night. It was, however, her first day back at school after a long summer – a day she would happily sleep through if not for the large seagull squawking outside her open window.

"*Gah!*" she shouted at the seagull. "I just need two more minutes before I—"

SQUAWK!

"Haven't you got anything better to do than bother a girl in her sleep?" Tetra murmured, wrapping her pillow around her ears and sinking her face into her mattress.

But, only a few seconds later, Tetra realised she should have known better than to tempt fate. And if not fate, then to tempt a seagull. To complain to a seagull was to encourage it even more so. Telling a seagull to leave the chips alone only makes it more hungry. Telling a seagull to be quiet only means an never-ending chorus of squawks.

And as it happened, the seagull by Tetra's window was feeling extra encouraged. Never before had it had this level of attention. It shuffled closer until its head poked through the open window, puffed up its chest, and with a might big breath...

SQUAWWKKKK!

"Shush, you squid for brains!" Tetra screamed one last time, hurling her pillow towards the window. The seagull was startled and it flew back towards the sea.

"You'd better hurry up," her mother called from another room. "Your porridge will get cold."

"Porridge again." Tetra sighed. "Nothing says first day back at school like a bowl of bland droop."

Tetra stumbled out of bed, with her dark, wavy hair slumped below her shoulders. Her bare feet dragged across the floor as she moved towards her bedroom door. Her bag was leaning against the wall near her door, barely zipped up, with more of her books sprayed across her floor than in the bag. Tetra looked at her bag with apprehension and sighed; today was not to be a day of adventure but a day stuck between the walls of a classroom.

School had never been a place Tetra enjoyed, nor a place she really felt welcome. She was free-willed and couldn't be moulded, with a stubbornness found only in the wildest of oceans. As an only child, with a father she could barely remember, she knew her dreams would have to be thrown in the bin as, one day, it would be her role to look after her mum like her own mother; traditions as predictable as the sun on a tropical paradise.

"Your porridge is now cold," her mother shouted from the other room.

Tetra slid around the corner and dropped herself down at the table. Her grandmother was already there, apparently blissfully eating her porridge too, while her mother was washing dishes in the basin.

"Did you feel the tremor?" her grandmother asked Tetra.

"Tremor?" Tetra replied, rolling her eyes.

"Yes, child, a book fell from m' shelf and landed on m' 'ead."

"I'm sure it was just a wonky shelf, I'll fix it later," said her mum.

"Listen 'ere, it wouldn't be the first tremor, mark m' words," said the grandmother.

"Why would that be?" asked Tetra.

"The sea has awoken. What took your dad many years ago has come back to take all of us!"

"We have no idea what happened to Jean," her mother interrupted.

"Sure, deny the world at your own peril," her grandmother said. "Believe me, there was a tremor and I've seen this all before…"

"Suddenly, I can't wait to go to school," Tetra said sarcastically, whilst pushing her bowl of porridge across the table and spinning out of her chair. She grabbed her bag and headed outside to face whatever the day would bring. It wasn't that she disliked her grandmother, nor did she dislike her mum, but she found the old ocean tales childish. How could the sea be any different than it was yesterday?

It was early in the morning. At such a time, the seagulls were always frantic, and today was no different. The seagull that had woken Tetra was back at her window, and as she walked past the seagull it stared back at her blankly.

"Thanks for waking me up," she told the seagull. "Did no one ever tell you it is rude to squawk so loudly at this time in the morning?"

The seagull looked back at her as it shuffled its feathers. It didn't seem bothered by her complaint, nor about anything else. It just wanted to perch on the side of her window and watch the world go by, its eyes turned towards the horizon, where the sea met the sky. Or, more importantly to Tetra, where the ships sailed away from the island.

It wasn't just the window dweller that was staring at the horizon. The seagull that sat on the wall and the other that stood on the pylon were staring at the sea too. Indeed, as Tetra walked away from her home and towards school, all the seagulls seemed to be staring towards the horizon. She could see nothing fascinating there though, only the same ships disappearing into the distance.

Even the wind felt the same, brushing against her face like it always did. Her hair flickered in the light breeze as she slowly walked her away along the stony path. Now aged ten, Tetra knew the island like a map in her mind, and she knew the seagulls were behaving particularly oddly today. Usually, seagulls did what seagulls always do. Wake you up, steal your chips, or take aim practice at your head. Her dad was the only person that liked them, at least from what she could remember. Apparently, he knew when he was closer to home after a long adventure with the sight of a seagull.

But, it was the first day of school and Tetra had little time to waste on stupid staring seagulls. She needed time to herself before she was crammed into a small classroom filled with other people. It wasn't that she disliked other children, indeed, some she would even consider friends, it was more that people made her tired. So tired, in fact, that she would often need to sit alone on the docks, watching the ships come and go.

"I wonder if my dad is still out there," she whispered to herself, staring out at the horizon from the docks. The waves crashed gently across each pylon, leaving not only salt, but the mixture of seaweed and crabs that lived in the shallows. Her legs dangled over the edge as small fish darted between each boat, silently weaving between the waves, leaving trails of bubbles in their wake.

Tetra stood up to watch a ship in the distance drawing closer and closer to the island. It wobbled aggressively for a few seconds and then steadied. But before she could wonder why, the dock she stood on shook violently, causing Tetra to fall onto her bottom.

"A tremor!" she whispered to herself. "Grandma hasn't lost all her marbles just yet."

She stood back up once more, and noticed the tide was moving away from the dock faster than it ever had before. Where the sea had once been were now layers of plastic waste and glass bottles, all sinking into the claws of the now bare seabed. As the tide moved closer and closer towards the horizon, it left a bare sand dune of filth and grime.

The white light of the sun danced against the backdrop of the horizon, there in the distance lay a pale strip between the sky and the sea. It grew with each breath that Tetra took. This was a phenomenon that Tetra had never seen before and, what was strangest of all, it was heading straight for her.

As the seagulls flocked together, blanketing the summer sky, what had seconds before been a mere white strip between the sky and the sea was now a wall of water, as tall as the mountain behind her.

Tetra stepped back in shock as the giant wave moved closer and closer towards the island, baring its teeth, snapping its way towards the shore. Soon enough, it was above Tetra and threatening to devour her and the rest of the island with it. Tetra stood alone as the wave fell on her with all its might; there was no umbrella in the world, nor even a boat, that could save her from the sea pouncing on her now.

In the final second, Tetra looked above to the sky, but there were no birds, nor were there lonely clouds passing by. Not even the sun could find its way through the thick, sea wall that was tumbling above her. Even when the light passed through the wave, there were no rainbows, only shadows casting darkness upon the island. And when the wave finally consumed the island, it had become a tsunami, crushing all that was in its way.

And when the island realised the destruction, Tetra was already gone.

Chapter 2
Neither Sunk Nor Afloat

Falling asleep was always easier for Tetra than waking up. The moment her eyes shut, another world would open. She could be exploring the jungles of Indonesia or island, hopping from Hawaii to Micronesia. But when she woke up, she would find herself back in bed on the island she had long dreamed about leaving.

But fate had a different plan that day. The moment she woke, she was neither in her bed nor on her island. In fact, where she was she hadn't seen in a book, nor had she felt in a dream. There was light glittering downwards, like the stars were falling around her. Her movements felt heavy, as if a great tide was moving against her. And there she was, being carried to a destination her imagination could not yet fathom.

Tetra's mind was dizzy. She felt two great forces working on her, one trying to pull her backwards and another trying to push her forwards. Every now and then, she would feel her body hit a great wall and then get pulled away again not a moment too soon. Then after some time, the world went dark again.

***

When Tetra woke once more, her movements felt less heavy. The same forces were attempting to hold her back, but this time they failed. She looked around and saw that she was lying on a wooden floor, each plank as uneven as the next. Her hand slid against the surface and it felt gritty, with a thick layer of salt covering it like compressed snow.

She tried to stand up, but when she did, she spun around and gently floated back down onto her bottom. She tried once more, only this time more slowly. When she arose, her feet were no longer touching the floor, hovering a good metre above it. She looked around to see a huge ship, not the biggest she had seen, but the biggest she had been on. It was, though, much emptier than it was large.

Much of the wood was rotting, with holes and cracks running across its length and breadth. There were three masts, each with sails that were torn and couldn't guide a paper boat down a gentle stream. And, on top, a flag, red with a golden castle painted in the middle. It couldn't flutter, it merely pointed towards the front of the ship and hopelessly sulked on its perch.

While the ship was strange, where it was and where it was going felt all the stranger. Above her were schools of fish swimming in the sky, and beneath her were more schools of fish swimming with the tide. It was as if the ship had neither sunk or swam, but lingered in between both a sunken and a floating ship.

Along with the waves above and the bubbles trickling from her mouth, Tetra realised she was somewhere she hadn't been before. And, if she was honest with herself, somewhere she shouldn't be at all.

"I'm under the sea," Tetra whispered, her eyes gliding across the surface above her. "How am I not drowning? This doesn't seem right at all."

Tetra swam cautiously to the surface, kicking her legs, just as she had been taught by her father, and looking down every now and then at the ship that hovered just below her. She reached out to touch the surface, but as her fingertips inched towards the open air, her hand was pushed back into the sea. She tried her other hand, and low and behold, her other hand was pushed back in the same way.

"You won't be getting out of here," a voice whispered from below. Tetra looked back down and saw the same empty ship that she had woken up on. There was no one there, nothing, not even a lonesome crab scuttling across the deck. She tried once more to break out of the sea, using more force than before. But just like before, her hand was pushed back into the sea.

"Doing the same thing twice often has the same consequences," a voice from below whispered once more, this time slightly louder. "It's also a little silly."

"Who's down there?" Tetra asked, with a slight shake on her upper lip.

There was no reply, at least not directly, though the planks near the bow of the ship could be heard creaking. She swam back towards the ship, checking the bow first before meandering her way towards its stern. But as her feet touched the deck, there was still no one, nothing, not even an octopus beneath the floor boards.

"Well, I know I'm not silly," Tetra said loudly across the ship.

Behind her, the cabin door rattled, and as it did, Tetra jumped off the ground and floated for what must have been five seconds before finding her nerve and turning to face the door, her eyes widening as she swallowed her fears. Then, silently, she crept towards the door. She reached out her hand and gently touched the brass handle.

"I wouldn't go in there if I were you," a voice whispered in her ear. She spun around to find two empty eyes staring back at her. She stumbled backwards, her heart beating through her skin, tumbling into barrels positioned beside the cabin door.

"I have the odd skeleton in my wardrobe," the voice said. "Besides, the captain's quarters are for me alone."

Tetra got back up to find a young man standing before her. He was just like her, only his hands and his legs seemed to disappear into the sea. His skin was as pale as the glaciers flowing into the cold northern seas, and he wore a blue jacket, much like the sailors in photographs from the olde days.

"Maybe I should introduce myself, I am Captain Neureus," the man said. "I, much like yourself, am trapped beneath the sea. Only I am less fortunate than you. While you have maintained your full body, I have mostly lost mine."

"What happened to you?" Tetra asked the captain.

"When one lives by the waves, one often dies by the waves," the captain chuckled.

"The wave! That's it!" Tetra muttered to herself. The captain's eyebrows rose as he stared at Tetra mumbling. "I was caught by a huge wave while I stood on the docks. Do you know how I can get back there?"

Captain Neureus stared at Tetra for a moment, then he grinned and turned towards the bow of the ship. He began to walk, or what seemed to be his way of walking, for with only sunken whispers for legs, he was mostly floating.

"There is only one way out of this ocean," the captain said, and Tetra followed him, waiting for the end of his sentence. After seconds that felt mostly like minutes to Tetra, they had reached the bow of the ship. They both stared out towards the open ocean. In the distance there appeared to be a forest, at least it would have been if it weren't below the sea. But there it stood, below the sea, a flourishing shadow of a forest, for all to see.

"Tell me then, how do I get out of here?" Tetra asked the captain.

"Ever seen a forest under the sea?" the captain asked Tetra.

"I have never seen anything under the sea until today," Tetra replied.

His cold, sunken eyes turned to face her, and behind him, Tetra caught the sight of the forest burning. She took a short breath, only to realise the forest was not burning but as green as it had been before. She raised an eyebrow, twitched her nose and then looked back towards the captain.

"And you might well remain here too, just like that forest, unless you can help me get my ship sailing again," the captain said.

"How am I supposed to do that?" Tetra asked. "This ship is such a wreck that it doesn't know whether to float or sink."

"That is mostly true," the captain chuckled. "However, I know how we can fix it, I just need you to collect me some items. I would get them myself; however, I am bound to my ship in more ways than one, a mere whisper of my former self. The shadow that a great man once cast."

"And you're sure this is the only way out of the ocean?" Tetra asked.

"I wouldn't say you're in a position to question it right now," the captain replied.

"All right." Tetra sighed. "What do you need?"

"Welcome aboard my ship," the captain chuckled. "Although, you won't be spending too much time on it. Within that forest in the distance" – the captain pointed once more towards the green silhouettes in the distance – "lies a wheel I need to get the ship moving again. So I would suggest you set sail to there first… or in your case, get swimming."

Tetra looked at the forest. It did not look welcoming. She exhaled loudly. "Well, I guess this is an adventure," Tetra said. "Although, not exactly what I had in mind."

"What kind of adventure could you have planned in your mind?" the captain asked. "You don't plan adventures, the wind merely carries you on one."

"That's exactly what my dad used to say," Tetra replied as she looked out towards the forest.

"The tide will carry you," the captain said. "Now, the sooner I have a wheel, the sooner we can get out of here. I would suggest you make like a kraken and get swimming."

Tetra put her hands on her hips. She was used to her mother bossing her around and even more so her teacher, but to be hurried up by some weird captain beneath the sea really felt like a new low point for her. However, it was her only way out of this strange new word, so with another sigh, she started to swim towards the forest. Once she was a good distance from the ship, she looked back at Captain Neureus, but he was no longer there.

Maybe he has returned to his cabin, Tetra thought.

But for now it didn't matter. There was a forest ahead, and if she wanted out of the ocean any time soon, she had better get there fast.

Chapter 3
Tangled up in Tentacles

Back home on Tetra's island, the trees were mostly shrubbish in nature. They had long, spindly trunks that grew taller than most of the island's buildings, all topped off with a flurry of large leaves that fought their way towards the sun. At the bottom of the sea, the trees didn't seem to grow towards the sun but flowed along with the tide.

The forest was still on the horizon. Along the way, dotted across the sandy bed, were trees that didn't quite look like trees, but must have been trees all the same. The tallest trees had green leaves that tickled the top of the surface, while the smallest trees had red leaves that gently caressed on the seafloor. The trees that grew in between didn't know what colour they wanted to be, as indecisive about their appearance as they were on their height. When Tetra slid her hand across their branches, they felt slimy, much like the seaweed that got caught between her toes on the beach back home. But unlike home, these trees danced, not just with the current forcing them to move, they were moving because they wanted to. The current was gentle, but they danced to a quicker, silent rhythm.

As Tetra swam between the trees, they seemed to wander with her, moving closer to her the deeper into their world she went. When she stopped, so did the trees. When she moved once more, they trees danced once again. When Tetra tapped her foot, the trees shook a branch, and when Tetra wiggled an arm, the trees would wiggle theirs. The trees were mimicking her, and it felt like mockery. She carried on swimming between them but now with a frown on her face.

"These are trees like none I have ever seen before," Tetra whispered to herself, whilst sliding her hand once more against a thin, blue leaf. It shuddered at her touch, curling up as she glided against its miry flesh.

As she looked back, Tetra saw that the ship was now a faint shadow in the distance, barely visible in the silent murk that lay on the horizon. The forest ahead looked even further though. In fact, it looked further away than it had when she stood on the bow of the ship. But there was only one way to go and that was to continue her journey forwards, so with another frown followed by half a smile, she carried on through the fields of slimy trees.

The silhouette of the ship finally disappeared behind her, and the shadows of the trees became larger and darker. Swimming between each tree was becoming more and more difficult as they danced towards her. The waves on the surface were steady, a silent pulse glided over the tips of the green leaves, but as the trees jittered and pranced, they clashed against the barrier that held everything beneath the sea.

Where she once had space to swim, Tetra now had to wiggle and wriggle between the hyperactive trees, struggling between each branch and stem that created room before closing behind her. Surrounded by the trees and darkness shrouding the distance, the forest ahead was now out of sight, and for the moment out of Tetra's mind.

Tetra sank to the bottom of the seabed and slumbered on a rock, exhausted and frustrated by the maze of trees that had been blocking every path she created. Her arms by now felt heavy and her legs weren't in much better shape. Her head sunk to her knees as she wondered what to do, her tears washing into the sea that drifted around the trees. She had never been this far from home before, and although she had dreamed of adventure, she always assumed she would be in control of what happened. At least, that's how every adventure she had ever read about seemed to be; a relentless hero storming a castle, with no slimy trees or disappearing forests to contend with.

"This is hopeless," Tetra whispered to herself, rolling a stone between her feet. "I'm lost on my first journey. This wasn't supposed to happen."

The current blew then like the wind on her hair, brushing each strand against her shoulders. It rattled against her ears, and as it did, there was a small voice carried inside its flow. It was faint, and the more Tetra focused on the words, the more unclear they became. She sighed, kicking her feet into the sand and drawing circles along the seafloor.

"Whatever the captain wants, he isn't getting at this point," Tetra said to herself, as the circles she had drawn in the sand slowly began to look like a shell, then a shell with flippers, and then a turtle gracefully gliding around the bottom of the sea. As the current turned, so did the turtle's shape, the sea washing streaks through its shell.

"These trees are weird," Tetra said to herself, as she lifted a branch from her shoulder. "They jiggle all by themselves and they won't stop trying to touch me."

Then the current pushed against her with much more force, nearly knocking Tetra off her rock. She grabbed onto the rock and pulled herself back up, floating just above the surface. The trees around her were jiggling more ferociously than before. Red leaves were stroking her toes and the large green ones were swirling above her.

It was the ones in between that were the most sinister, though. One tried wrapping itself around Tetra's arm, but she was quick and pushed it away. She began to swim away but another grabbed her ankle and started pulling her in. Tetra screamed, flailing her legs as hard as she could until it let go. Then she closed her eyes and swam until she could swim no more, kicking her legs and wailing her arms until she fumbled over another rock and bounced onto the sand. She opened her eyes, still surrounded by trees that were edging towards her.

On the ground in front of her, a clam shell lay vacant. Looking closer, it was vacant because it was broken. Where it was broken, it looked sharp. Not sharp like a knife but sharp enough to cut through leaves. She waved it towards the trees and they halted.

"Go away," she growled at the trees.

"I would love to," said a voice from behind the trees. "The pwoblem is, I'm stuck."

"Who's there?" said Tetra, pointing the clam shell higher, her heart thumping faster than the fist of a lobster.

"Is that you, Odis?" said the voice once more. "If it is, I don't find this amoosing any more. I'm weally hungwee."

"Odis?" retorted Tetra. "I'm not Odis whoever, or whatever Odis might be."

Tetra moved forward and as she did, the trees slowly danced away from her, revealing a tangle of intertwined branches curling around each other. From inside the tangled mess, a flipper poked out, one as scaly as a lizard's sun-kissed belly, with small algae growing between the cracks.

"You not Odis?" the voice said. "Well, can you help an ol' pal out and pull me out anyway?"

Tetra put the clam down, grabbed the enormous flipper and began to pull, and pull and pull. She pulled until her arms ached and her fingers were sore. But the flipper was enormous and her hands were so little they could barely grip. It also didn't help that the flipper jiggled more than the trees themselves.

"Can't you keep still?" said Tetra, her face as red as the sun was hot.

"I can't help it," the voice chuckled. "Your fwippers are so tickwish."

"I don't have flippers," squeaked Tetra, out of breath from all the pulling. "I have hands."

"Hands?" asked the voice. "Like fins?"

"No, like hands," said Tetra, now not pulling as her arms were aching from her shoulders to her finger tips. "I'm sorry, you're too big. I can't pull you out."

"Well, that's unfowunate," murmured the voice. "Thwanks for your time anyway."

"I think I can—"

"I'll never taste a jellyfwish again," said the voice. "Maybe not even a wittle one."

"But I think I can—"

"What I would do for a jellyfwish."

Tetra sighed, picked up the broken clam and began slicing the vines one by one. All the while the strange creature whittled on about jellyfish, which made it seem even stranger. Jellyfish were gross. And if you got too close to them, they had a bad habit of stinging.

Tetra sliced through the kelp with more ease than she had expected. Soon the flipper was free to wiggle, then as she cut through, another flipper appeared.

"I can move my fwippers," beamed the voice. "What sowcery is this?"

"Just a sharp clam," said Tetra.

"Dewicious clams are," said the voice. "I had one just befwore I got stwuck in here."

After a short while, out of all the tangle, a creature emerged that perhaps she should have expected. An enormous turtle, with young eyes but an old face, glided gracefully out from the darkness he had once been in. Its shell had green and purple algae growing between its cracks, while its flippers were as big as Tetra was tall.

"Thanks sew much," gleamed the turtle. "They call me Tantalus. I don't know why."

Chapter 4
Jelly in the Belly

Tetra's grandma always used to say that turtles came to the island in their thousands when she was little. But Tetra had never believed it. Thousands on a small island seemed ridiculous to her. She had seen many swim past the island but only a few had ever landed on the beach itself. Now Tetra wondered if maybe many turtles getting themselves tangled up in kelp was the cause of their disappearance from the island.

"Haven't seen a merwaid down here before," said Tantalus. "Ugely, you hear storwies of them, but now I weally did meet one."

"A mermaid? Me?" Tetra questioned. "How could you possibly think I'm a mermaid?"

"Well, you sure do look like a merwaid," answered Tantalus, inspecting her closely. "And you couldn't be a sirwen because you don't have evil eyes."

"Mermaids and sirens are not real," retorted Tetra. "Though actually, I'm not sure if any of this is real yet. I mean, how could I possibly be under sea with a talking turtle?"

"Turtles have always been able to tawk," chuckled Tantalus. "At weast to each other."

"So, I'm a turtle now?" asked Tetra, raising her eyebrow.

"No," said Tantalus, turning upside down with his flippers behind his head. "I would say, if you're not a merwaid or a sirwen, maybe you're some kind of hairwess seal."

"Nope, definitely not a seal."

Tantalus rested his flipper on his chin, all the while gliding upside down, and looked at Tetra with his big, blue eyes. He then rubbed his head, opened his gaping mouth, only to close it again seconds later.

"*Hmmm,*" Tantalus hummed. "Maybe, some kind of otter."

"Nope, not an otter," Tetra said as she pointed to her cheeks, "I don't have whiskers."

"*Hmmm,*" hummed Tantalus once more. Tetra looked at him with slight bemusement. She had met some silly people in her time, even some silly seagulls, but a silly turtle was completely new to her.

"Maybe a walking starwish," he finally said.

"A walking starfish?" Tetra repeated, her frown now looking like a deep-sea trench. "That is the most ridiculous thing I've ever heard, and believe me, I've heard some silly stuff."

Tetra swam faster, winding through the great gaps now between each tree. She glanced behind to see the turtle closely following, still upside down with his head towards the clouds. Even when she paddled with all her might, Tantalus could match her speed with one swoop of a great flipper.

"Def not a starwish," said Tantalus. "They don't swim like that."

"Look," said Tetra sternly, turning around to face the turtle. "Why do you insist on following me?"

"You saved me fwom the giant kelp twees," said Tantalus. "I owe you some kindness in retuwn."

"By laughing at how I swim?" Tetra said with her hands now firmly on her hips.

"I was not laffing," said the turtle, waving his flippers around. "I was just cuwious about you."

"Well, if you must know, I'm human," said Tetra, slowly

glancing her eyes up to the surface. "Or at least I used to be."

Tantalus rubbed his flipper on his chin some more, his eyes staring away from Tetra. He hummed some more, before rubbing his belly, then glanced back at Tetra.

"I think I'm 'ungry," he finally said. "Where we 'eading anyway?"

"We?" questioned Tetra, turning around and paddling forwards once more.

"Sure," said the turtle, closely following behind. "I owe you, wemember?"

"Think nothing of it."

"I can't do that, you swaved my life."

"I'm on an adventure too far away from here."

"To where?"

"The forest up ahead."

"The Malign Mangwove?" shuddered the turtle, twisting his neck towards his shell. "I wouldn't adwenture too close to there. Perhaps your holiday destinawion should be somewhere more comfwotable. The colours of the weef might be more to your tastes, although they have been looking a wittle pale wecently. Or maybe the Fawaway Lagoon that actually isn't that fawaway, or—"

"Stop," Tetra interrupted, with her frown once more painted across her face. "I need to go to this forest and find a wheel for the ship which will get me out of here."

"Ship? I haven't seen a ship around here."

"Well, there is one."

"Why would there be a wheel in the fowest?"

"I don't know!" Tetra yelled, raising her hands in the air and back down again, quicker than a seagull could flap its wings. Tantalus fell silent, and as it happened, so did Tetra. They continued weaving through the kelp leaves towards nowhere, but as always happens, nowhere always leads to somewhere.

They wound through the stems, the leaves hiding them like a chest hides its gems. Their adventure was a slow one, not only because of all the kelp trees, but also because a human really couldn't move easily beneath the sea. She paddled through like a dog in a pond, struggled through the current like a leaf in the wind, and pushed through the sea like a starfish pursuing a swordfish.

Soon, they had woven their bodies through much of the kelp and an opening was forming in front of them. Now, just in front of the horizon was the forest she had seen from back on the ship. In between the kelp and the forest was a small, empty dune, with shallow domes dotted around.

"We can still turn bwack if you would pwefer the lagoon," Tantalus said, tilting his head in her direction.

"Nope, got to find that wheel," Tetra replied, her eyes focussing on the mangrove in the near distance. Tetra began to swim with much determination. The murk of the forest didn't deter her, nor did it seem to scare her. Nothing could stand in her way now… until something did! She was bounced back by a force so squidgy, so gelatinous, that she was propelled into a backflip.

"What is this?" Tetra stammered.

"If I didn't know better, I would say…" But before Tantalus could finish his words, a translucent blob arose from the ground like a balloon escaping the atmosphere. As it rose, so did the tentacles that hung beneath it, kicking up a mist of sand in the eyes of both Tetra and Tantalus.

Tetra pushed backwards, away from the cloud of sand, and looked up towards the surface of the sea. There, blanketing much of the open space was perhaps the biggest creature she had ever seen. She was sure it was even bigger than the ones she had read about.

"A j-jellyfish," she stuttered, her eyes widening and her lips wavering. "But it's massive."

"I know!" Tantalus said, visibly drooling and slowly moving

towards the head of the jellyfish.

"What are you doing?" Tetra yelled. "That jellyfish could kill us with one zap of its tentacle."

"Consider us even now," Tantalus chuckled, with more drool streaming from his mouth. "This could be the biggwest dinner I've had in weeks!"

"Dinner?" Tetra yelled once more. "How can that jellybeast possibly be dinner?"

"Watch and wearn, my fwiend," said Tantalus, and he swooped towards the giant jellyfish. He dived into the gelatinous beast, and then emerging as quickly as he had entered, with more jelly in his mouth than he should be able to swallow. After several more bites, its tentacles arose to try and fight back, but by the time they reached the turtle, the deed was done and the giant jellyfish seemed to deflate, sinking into the sand before Tetra's eyes.

A deflated balloon would have had more dignity than the jellyfish after Tantalus was done with it, but as it drifted away in the current like a plastic bag in the wind, it dawned on Tetra that there would likely be more coming. She swam out cautiously into the opening; the forest loomed near, and although she dreaded the forest and all its gloom, she knew the captain was eagerly awaiting a ship's wheel.

"Are there any more?" Tetra called out to Tantalus, as he sunk to the seabed with his eyes shut and his flippers on his belly.

"Pwobably," Tantalus yawned. "But my belly can wait for them in the morning."

"Are you just going to lie there?"

"No… maybe…" Tantalus debated with himself. "Ah yes, yes. Here is a good place to nap and west an old shell's belwy."

"Fine," said Tetra, with her nose in the air and turning her back on Tantalus. "I can find this wheel on my own."

"You really shouldn't go in the forwest," said Tantalus, now lying on the sand with his flippers behind his head. "Most fwish that enter never come back out again."

"Good thing I'm not a fish then," Tetra said slowly drifting towards the forest. But up ahead of her, she could see more giant jellyfish lying across the seabed like land mines, blocking the entrance. So, sneaking in the way an octopus would, only not quite as invisible and not quite as agile, Tetra approached.

Although the jellybeasts themselves were visibly snoring, if that's what jellybeasts could do, they occasionally shuffled and bumped as if they might wake at any moment. The tentacles swung randomly like a bus caught in a tornado, snapping at the sand, and when one tentacle hit another, it would sizzle like a hot pan in cold water. Sometimes, it was as if the tentacles had a mind of their own, like a hydra with several heads vying for a mouthful of flesh. One slammed behind Tetra, only inches away from her, and the sand beneath it turned to glass. Another tentacle, not quite as large but large nonetheless, tickled the ground in front of her, sliding like a burying eel. Tetra's hair sizzled as another tentacle waved over it. Fortunately, being undersea, it cooled quickly enough not to leave her bald, just with a little extra curl.

She looked back to see she was already halfway there. In the distance, Tantalus was fast asleep on the back of his shell, large bubbles rising from his mouth. She looked around and saw more sleeping jellybeasts, all snoring just as much as Tantalus. She gulped and moved slowly forward.

"I can do this," she murmured to herself, with images of her first time on a bouncy castle flashing through her mind, young Tetra jumping between the ricocheting bodies of her friends as they dashed away from the collapsing castle. To be trapped inside would have been devastating, but to be tangled in the tentacles of a jellybeast would be so much worse.

But the current pushed her forward between each great jelly

beast, easing her ride through the passage. Before she knew it, her hands had grasped the branch of a tree in the mangrove. As she looked back, the great jelly beasts were still fast asleep, and beyond them, so was Tantalus, lounging in his own gluttony. But that was now behind her and as the dark walls of the mangrove opened like a secret door, so did Tetra's determination to find the wheel.

Chapter 5
The Sound of a Light

The tide brushed the leaves of the trees like the wind did on land. There was life in the forest, but it rarely moved, trapped by the walls of the trees or tucked beneath the bark with little room to swim. Strangely, the water was shallower than it had been before, but little seemed to flow in, and if Tantalus had been correct, the forest would let very little out. But Tetra had no time to worry about his words; she had a captain waiting for a wheel.

She crept between the trees, under their mangled roots and over their dampened bodies. Her feet gently kicked against the sea and her hands guided her through the obstacles that the forest presented. The water felt grainy, like it was carrying dirt or sand along with it. Even when some light found its way through the thick canopy, Tetra could only see a few metres in front of her. But when she did get to see something, even a leaf or a small snail, Tetra wished she hadn't.

Some of the trees had faces, at least so it seemed. Tetra couldn't be sure whether the trees were smiling or grimacing at her. Trees shouldn't have faces, she decided. Tetra hoped it was just her imagination, but sunken holes in the bark had a weird way of following her every movement. Even the fungi that grew on the trees' battle-hardened bodies had moments where they seemed more jellyfish than mushroom, glowing to reveal small paths between the thick bushes.

One path led to another, and where one path stopped, another three would start. Every tree looked different, but also remarkably similar. They had to be related, like one giant family that had settled in the same place centuries before.

If the dancing kelp trees had been disorienting, then the forest was a maze where the entrance and exit changed at random. Or at its worst, a bottle that had been plugged, Tetra thought, leaving her trapped inside. But Tetra's frown was beginning to waver. What had been two eyebrows in a V shape was now two eyebrows almost touching her hairline. Her eyes had widened, and her breathing became heavy, although few bubbles left her mouth.

"I swear I passed this tree before," she whispered to herself. "No, that other tree had more mushrooms. Maybe it's this way…" Tetra stumbled further into the shadows, and when she was in a deeper shadow, she stumbled into the shadows' shadows. Even the light was dark, and when it shone, it tapped the trees like a crab cracking a shell.

The mushrooms were now swarming like jellyfish. Oddly, they could swim, and they did so in the same direction, and whether Tetra liked it or not, she was compelled to go with them too. Through the thick foliage, and between the gaps of branches, Tetra and mushrooms swam through a small opening.

Small fragments of light trickled down like drizzle on a Spring day. The opening allowed the light to bounce between the leaves and find its way to the seabed, which was much more like mud than the glistening sand it had been outside the forest.

A large snail, with a shell as speckled as the moon, slithered through the mud towards a light patch of red seaweed that lay dormant on the floor. It ignored Tetra; didn't even raise its head to look at her. It was perhaps the only thing in the forest that didn't notice Tetra. The whispers between the trees were getting louder and Tetra had the horrible feeling they might be about her. She pressed on, nonetheless.

The small opening soon became a narrow path, and the narrow path led to a small meadow in which were beautiful flowers that Tetra had never seen before. The petals resembled the waves themselves, flowing majestically with the calm current that tickled across the sand.

Where the flowers didn't grow, the light grass appeared brown, if not sometimes black. Tetra stroked her hand across the blades and it crumbled into the sand, leaving a murky haze in the water.

As Tetra slowly floated through the meadow, watching the snails munch their way to a bellyache, a loud bang jolted her into a spin. After the third spin, she settled and looked around to see a grey cloud rising from one of the trees on the edge of the meadow.

She gently paddled towards the tree to find a hole had been zapped all the way through it. It looked fried around the edges, and if that wasn't bad enough, the smell resembled her mother's cooking.

"There's a smell I'd hoped I could forget," she murmured to herself, twinging her nose away from the hole. "How could something burn underwater?"

She glanced around and could see nothing out of the ordinary, or out of the ordinary for a strange forest under the sea. She placed her hands on her hips and sighed, then began to paddle towards the centre of the meadow where a patch of purple flowers were dancing in the current.

Before she could paddle two metres more, there was another loud bang in front of her. More ash rose, and the trees to her left moved like a wave rolling over the surface. Through a large gap between the trees, sharp teeth, as big as Tetra's arm, darted towards her.

Tetra swam towards the forest as fast as she could. The teeth were faster though and were catching up fast. When she looked behind, she saw that the creature resembled a massive eel with a long jaw and electric sparks sizzling around its body. Its fins were tiny, like a lizard had lost its legs… or a snake. It seemed to be an electric snake under the sea.

The electric beast opened its large jaw and just as it snapped, Tetra rolled into the forest and out of its way. She continued paddling as fast as she could between the trees. From behind, she could hear electric jolts zapping into trees and the smell had worsened: this time much nastier than her mum's cooking.

She wiggled through until she arrived through a wider opening, which led to a larger meadow. As she stumbled past the last tree, she noticed this meadow had a statue that stood so tall until it tickled the surface.

The statue was made from a dark marble and glistened a dark glow under the sun. It had five heads which resembled fish but with hundreds of dragon teeth. The five heads each had their own long neck which grew from the same body. There were four webbed claws that looked as sharp as harpoons, and great fins as large as dinghies. And there, in one of the mouths, Tetra saw a wooden wheel, with large handles for steering.

"That must be the ship's wheel," Tetra gasped, raising her hands in the air. She began swimming towards it, but a large boom from behind stopped her in her path. She snuck behind the statue, peeping out with just one eye, and saw the electric beast zoom out of the forest, swirling with even more electricity than before.

It zoomed around in front of the statue, sparking jolts into the ground, leaving scorch marks all over the meadow. The flowers began to close, trying to hide from the burn of its electricity, but it made no difference, they were fried too.

The electric beast gave out a roar that made the trees shudder, and even made Tetra curl up and whimper behind the statue. She didn't like to admit it, but she was terrified. She lowered herself onto the sand, and stayed there, trying to calm herself, for ten seconds, before taking another glance.

Now there was nothing in the meadow but scorch marks. Not a sound, nor a whisper. She peeked her other eye out and still saw nothing. She sighed in relief and paddled a little, but regretted it instantly. On the other side of the statue, two green eyes were staring at her.

BZZZ! A jolt came and zapped the statue. Small pieces of marble tumbled down to the sand as the great electric beast came swimming towards Tetra. She whirled back behind the statue, but now the beast knew where she was and followed.

They both darted upwards, swirling around the statue, the electric beast zapping as they swam. When they reached one of the heads, the beast zapped, and as the current crackled through the water, it dislodged the wheel and it fell from the mouth of the five-headed statue.

Tetra watched as the wheel sank to the ground, and when she looked in the direction the electric beast was, it was gone. Only a trail of disturbed trees could be seen in the distance, but Tetra could hear the faint sound of whimpering.

She looked back at the wheel and had begun swimming down towards it when a snarl stopped her. She looked back to see that the head that once held the wheel was suddenly very much alive and very much angry. Soon the other heads were moving too, and a small crack that ran down the body of the statue was getting larger.

Chapter 6
Five Heads Ahead

The wheel lay flat on the seabed, algae growing between its handles and splinters cracking at its sides. Tetra picked it up and stared at it; a smile gleaming across her face. But the smile didn't last for long. Behind her, the crack in the statue was growing by the second and the five heads were snarling in her direction.

Clutching the wheel, she swam as hard as she could. Swimming fast was hard though, especially for a human who hadn't been under the sea for long. The weight of the wheel made it all the more difficult, and instead of swimming like an acrobatic dolphin, she struggled like a wounded lobster, kicking the sand up as she went. But she managed to drag herself out of the meadow and through the winding trees and bushes. A swarm of mushrooms rushed past her. They were much faster than they had been before, and, as if by some kind of strange sorcery, they appeared more jellyfish-like. They certainly weren't the glowing mushrooms they had been when Tetra originally entered the forest.

The forest had also changed. It had been a maze before, with strange paths leading towards the statue. But now, even the paths had disappeared, becoming a mist of wood and branches, smothering both the sky and the seabed.

Tetra stumbled through, guided by the fading glow of the mushrooms and motivated by the growling behind her. She stumbled and tumbled, tripping over one log and ducking under another, until she came to another meadow, this one much smaller than the one before.

She stopped and her eyes widened. In the middle was a huge gathering of mushrooms, all glowing dimly. They were growing, and they all grew until they were about twice the size of Tetra. And when they stopped growing, their glow faded, and they began to rise above the trees, their small tentacles dragging across the leaves.

"Baby jelly beasts," Tetra whispered, her eyes widening until they absorbed all the light from the rising moon. "It's getting dark, I need to get out of—"

Before she could finish her sentence, another loud roar came from behind her. She turned to see at least four trees snap in the distance and a huge head rise above the canopy.

"The statue," Tetra sighed. "It's found me."

The head snapped at the rising jelly beasts, gouging on as many as it could before another head came out of the forest and growled at it. Soon, another three heads appeared, all growling at each other, fighting over the jelly beasts. As Tetra tried to slowly make her escape, one of the heads noticed her and snarled. Then the other four heads turned to face her, and the whole beast came marauding towards her.

Tetra turned and made a dash for the forest, but the forest was wilder than it had been before. Roots were rising from the ground and shrivelling until they crumbled, and before she knew what was happening, one had lifted her high into the sea, leaving her at the exact height of an enormous head.

The hydra stared at Tetra, floating in the middle of the meadow, with her hands clutched onto the wheel. Bubbles drifted out of the hydra's nose and popped as they hit the surface of the sea. It curled up its lips, showed its long, barbed teeth which dripped red like a flame the sea could not extinguish. Tetra gulped. The hydra's eyes suddenly narrowed and it turned to look at another one of its heads, then it roared until the forest rumbled. The force of its roar propelled Tetra backwards, where her back slammed against a tree and the wheel fell onto her lap.

Tetra raised her head once more, looked towards the meadow and saw the five heads slowly moving towards her. She gritted her teeth, and locked her gaze onto the middle head's eyes for about three seconds, before darting behind the tree and moving silently out of its sight. She lifted the wheel up in front of her face and tried to hold her breath as she heard the sound of nostrils sniffing against the sand.

Tetra felt each breath from the hydra coming closer from five different directions. She could hear the sound of trees being crushed as the enormous body pushed through the forest and knocked the agitated roots out of its way. Each snarl, each growl, each thud was a moment closer than it had been before. Tetra had to get out of the forest and back to the ship without the hydra noticing her. She kept close to the seabed and crept like a crab from tree to tree.

And then, there was light at the end of the darkness. Between the whirling trees and temperamental roots was a large opening, one that looked familiar. Behind her, the hydra could still be heard snapping and snarling around the collapsing forest. She pushed towards the light, clutching the wheel tightly, and found herself back at the small opening where an enormous turtle lay sleeping.

"Tantalus!" Tetra cried at the top of her voice. "We have got to get out of here!"

Tantalus awakened, with his flippers still clutched to his belly. Before he could murmur 'jelly' one more time, he spun around with a jolt and faced a forest that now looked like a war zone.

"Well, this is a pwoblem," he said as Tetra came swimming as fast she could straight at him. "Oh, but you found a wheel," Tantalus said with a smile on his face.

"Yes, no time to talk," Tetra yelled with a shortness in her breath. "We have got to get out of here before the hydra destroys us too."

As she spoke, a large tree snapped and floated past her and one of the heads of the hydra peered over the canopy, watching her swim towards the kelp.

"Best jump on my shwell," Tantalus said. "I can swim just a wittle bit faster than you." He turned his back to face Tetra and she jumped on with both her hands clasping the rough surface and the wheel lodged between her arms. Tantalus dived deep into the kelp and away from the forest. In the distance, the silhouette of the five heads could be seen terrorising the forest, while its loud screeches could still be felt as harshly as they had in the meadow.

"How did you upset the hydwa?" Tantalus asked Tetra.

"I didn't," she retorted. "It upset itself. I was minding my own business when an electric beast attacked me and zapped a statue. Then before I knew it, the statue turned into that beast behind me!"

"I'm sure the Hydwa will calm down soon," said Tantalus, snorting a small chuckle. "You know, I heard the best jellyfwish come from the forwest."

"The hydra certainly enjoyed them," muttered Tetra.

"I hear they're so dewicious even the twees themselves eat the jellyfwish,"

After a while, he paused and turned around to face the forest. They were now amongst the kelp trees, but even they had stopped dancing and began to slowly slump and wilt. Tetra stared out at the forest and noticed an orange glow hanging behind the silhouette of the forest.

"I've heard about fire," said Tantalus. "I heard under the sea it was impwossible. I guess the hydwa really is angwy."

Tetra started at the wheel and a tear fell from her left eye. Another tear was about to fall from her right eye but decided to hurry back into her eye socket instead. She took one last look at the fire devouring the forest and tapped Tantalus on his shoulder.

"Let's go," she whispered. "The captain is waiting for his wheel."

Tantalus slowly turned around, and moved through the kelp that now detached from the comfort of the seabed with only a slight nudge. The kelp rose to the surface and clattered against the barrier, where it drifted with the tide over the horizon.

Soon, the ship was in their sight and Tantalus carried her carefully towards the bow of the vessel that neither floated or sunk. Tetra, gripping the wheel, beamed with happiness. She couldn't wait to show the captain what she had found and start her journey back home.

Chapter 7
Bones to Pick

The ship rattled and bounced as the current swirled around it like a timid tornado. It hovered like it had before, unable to sink or float, just sort of lingering in suspense. The same wooden planks squeaked, the same ragged flag fluttered, and the same cabin door still tempted Tetra.

"Where's this captain of yours?" asked Tantalus.

"He's here, he's here..." Tetra replied. "Last time, he appeared when I tried to open the door."

"Maybe you should twy opening it again then," said Tantalus.

"I don't know," said Tetra. "Last time, the captain was quite upset about it."

"You didn't mind upsetting the hydwa back there," Tantalus replied with a wry smile. Tetra stopped swimming and Tantalus soon stopped too. She looked into his eyes with more force than the electric beast could emit from its veins, and a frown that crinkled deeper than the darkest trenches.

"I did not upset the hydra," Tetra exclaimed. "The hydra upset itself. I was merely in the crossfire of unfortunate events."

Tetra and Tantalus turned to face the forest in the far distance, where the silhouette of five heads could be seen fighting amongst themselves. And there, where the trees once stroked the surface of the sea, there was an untamed flame that not even the sea could cool.

"Won't be long before the hydwa reaches the kewlp," Tantalus gulped. "This home of yours, does it have warm sandy beaches?" Both Tetra and Tantalus turned to swim towards the cabin door once more.

"It sure does," Tetra replied. "Why do you ask?"

"Oh, no reason." Tantalus chuckled and then gulped once more. "I'm sure this ol' turwtle will be fine here."

Tetra sunk her head low, unable to look Tantalus in the eye. She found herself swimming slower, and soon found herself swimming so slow that a sea slug sliding across the deck had overtaken her. She looked back up at Tantalus who was now a few strokes in front of her.

"Tantalus?" asked Tetra. Tantalus looked back with a wry smile. "Where are the other turtles?"

"I have no idea," Tantalus replied. "One by one, the others simpwy vanished."

"Vanished?" asked Tetra. "But how? How can they just vanish?" Tantalus merely shrugged with his flippers above his head. His smile soon disappeared, and he turned back towards the cabin door.

"Well, here's the dwoor," said Tantalus. "I wonder if something dewicious awaits us."

"Your bellied rumbled," said Tetra.

"I know."

"Wasn't the jelly beast enough?"

"Yes. At the time."

They approached the door quietly, but when they got there, they found the door already slightly open by less than an inch. Tantalus nudged Tetra forward, and as she tumbled a little towards the door, she steadied and took a big gulp.

"Well, here goes nothing," she whispered to herself. Tetra slowly pushed the door wider, and, when her head could fit through the gap, she peered through. A flickering lamp rattled on the ceiling, and a large oak table with rounded corners and chunky legs stood proudly on top a large rug; a chair turned and faced a window so grimy that the sea outside couldn't be seen.

"Captain?" Tetra whispered, creeping her first two toes through, followed by her second and her third. "Are you there?"

"Is he there?" whispered Tantalus, trying to peer his own head around the corner of the door.

"I don't think so," Tetra whispered back, with her second foot catching up with the first.

She glanced around some more and saw shelves filled with soggy paper, where words had long ago melted into the sea. In the middle of one shelf lay a bottle, and inside the bottle lay a ship, and as Tetra swam closer, she saw the ship had long tentacles wrapped around it.

Tetra placed the wheel next to the shelf and reached to pick up the bottle as gently as she could. She peered at the tentacles, and the closer she peered, the more alive they became. She turned the bottle around to look underneath the ship, and there staring back were two bulging eyes. She gasped and a small octopus flew out of the bottle. And when she looked around the cabin to find the octopus once more, it had already vanished, or at best hidden somewhere else.

On the other side of the room a large globe lay on the floor, slightly cracked on the Pacific Ocean. It was a strange globe, nothing like Tetra had ever seen before. The land was a dark obsidian colour while the seas remained vibrant, with different pastels of blue. Tetra tried to find her island on the globe but only found a small hole instead, perfectly cut in the shape of her island. She looked at Tantalus and he responded with a shrug.

Tetra crept slowly towards the large oak table in the centre of the room as Tantalus drifted close behind. When she swam above it, she could see a large map which looked as pristine as any map outside of the sea. When Tetra ran her hand across it, it didn't feel wet nor did it tear, it felt as dry as her school textbooks.

Upon closer inspection, the map wasn't exactly like the globe. Rather than a sphere, the world was shaped like a bottle. In the middle was an island shaped like a ship, and at the end where the bottle concaved, there was an island that looked like a giant octopus. There were various other strange islands, one shaped as a whale and another that almost resembled a hydra. At this point, Tetra wasn't sure if it was a map or a children's drawing.

"Stwange map," Tantalus said. "I find it much easier to simply wander in one diwection and find out where the sea intends me to be."

"That sounds like a good way to get lost," Tetra replied.

"Sure, but you find the most dewicious jellyfwish when you're lost. Some flavours you never knew existed."

"All the better reason to have a map," Tetra said and then rolled her eyes. "I've seen enough jellyfish for one day and don't to want to swim into more. I wonder what this map means though. I can't figure it out."

"I don't know," Tantalus shrugged. "Your captwain looks like he was last here five-hundwed years ago. We should probably make like a jelly and wiggle away."

Tetra and Tantalus made their way to the door, Tetra was feeling frustrated that Captain Neu-reus was nowhere to be seen. By now, the sun was fading in the sky, and bright colours of orange and pink raged through the darkening sky. Each beam of light trickled through the door that was now wide open for the whole ocean to see.

Behind them, a sudden swoosh creaked through their ears like a seagull sweeping down to steal their lunch. Tetra and Tantalus turned their heads sharply and behind them the chair had turned to face them and in it sat a skeleton. They both froze with their mouths wide open. The skeleton's head was slumped on the desk and both its hands grasped onto the map.

"Five-hundwed years old?" Tantalus said with sudden heavy breaths. "I think maybe a thousand years old."

"Well, he doesn't look like he's in a hurry to go anywhere," said Tetra, slowly backing away as the wheel trembled in her hands.

"His chair did turn awound all by itself," said Tantalus.

Tetra hovered with her hands on her hips, staring at the skeleton. It wore a blue tunic with white buttons, and a red vest underneath. The captains in books had hats though, and this skeleton for all its pompous extravagance, did not have a hat. Indeed, a hat may have been useful, for the top of its skull had a slight fracture.

"Nope, definitely dead," said Tetra.

"You ever seen a dead person tap his fwinger like that?" Tantalus stammered.

"I'm sure it's just the—" Before Tetra could finish, the skeleton raised its head and stared back at them. A cold current swept through Tetra's hair and down her neck. Even her voice froze, and when she tried to whisper, a mere bubble floated out her mouth and popped on the ceiling.

By the time Tetra could move, the skeleton had already risen to its bony feet and unsheathed a rusty sword that looked as brittle as the bones he staggered on. His once empty eye sockets were now a violent green and his few teeth chattered against the water. He approached Tetra and Tantalus, and as the last light of sunlight faded, his glowing eyes grew meaner.

Chapter 8
The Spirit Beneath the Bones

Moonlight blazed through the gap in the door, casting the skeleton's shadow against the grimy window. As the skeleton raised its sword, the shadow raised its sword even higher, touching the ceiling and reaching almost above the rest of the room. Both Tetra and Tantalus jumped in opposite directions, with Tetra swimming towards the globe and Tantalus diving towards one of the shelves.

"I told you I had a skeleton in my wardrobe," said a voice. "Quite literally, actually."

Tetra turned towards the voice and found Captain Neureus leaning back in the chair, with his feet up on the table.

"Help us!" Tetra yelled to Captain Neureus. "I got your wheel, see?" She held up the wheel with both hands and turned her face towards the skeleton which was slowly lumbering towards her.

"And you did a fine job," Captain Neureus said. "However, I haven't been in control of this skeleton for a long time. He has a mind of his own now. Well… what's left of his mind."

"So, you're just going to sit there?" Tetra yelled, as the skeleton lumbered closer and closer, raising his sword once more.

"There's really not much I can do," said Captain Neureus as he stretched his arms behind his head.

The skeleton's rusty sword hung above Tetra's head like a guillotine waiting to fall. But just when it was time for the sword to plunge downwards, it did not. Instead, the skeleton that had been one split into several pieces, and as each bone drifted away from another, a large turtle came crashing through the remnants of the undead sailor.

"There," said Tantalus. "You should never turn your back on a turwtle."

"Why did you do that for?" cried Captain Neureus, who was now stood up over the desk. "It will take me hours to put myself back together."

"Yourself?" yelled Tetra, as she turned and scowled at the captain.

"Who else would be sat in the captain's chair in the captain's cabin?" said Captain Neureus.

"So, if he's you, how are you both separated?" asked Tetra, clutching tightly onto the wheel.

"It's a long story," Captain Neureus replied. "Let's take a walk outside the cabin."

Tetra, Tantalus and Captain Neureus headed out of the door and across the deck of the ship. Now with the moon so high in the sky, it glimmered silver across the surface, and schools of fish shone like gems as they rose from the depths. In the distance, the fires of the forest had now faded but the five heads of the hydra could still be seen fighting amongst themselves as they slowly drifted towards the kelp.

"Have you ever heard of a kraken?" Captain Neureus asked Tetra.

"Oh no, not more mythical stories," Tetra said, rolling her eyes.

"*Gah,*" the captain protested. "Every myth has some truth to it. I bet you never believed in hydras until today?"

"No," Tetra murmured with her head sunk towards the deck.

"What about undead skeletons?" asked the captain. "I bet you never thought they could come to life when the moon rises?"

"No," Tetra replied once more.

"Or those giant jellyfwish?" said Tantalus with his tongue leaving his mouth and his flippers placed on his belly.

"Yeah, yeah… that too," said the captain. "So, in the world where you are now, krakens could be very real. Perhaps they are even more real than you and I. Maybe actually, a human that can live under the sea is the most peculiar creature here?"

"That's fair," admitted Tetra.

They arrived at the bow of the ship where they stared out towards a forest that barely existed any more.

"The hydra is one beast that I have never faced," said the captain. "But by the looks of it, with only five heads, it will surely be easier to tame than a kraken with its hundreds of tentacles. The kraken is why me and the skeleton are now apart. We were once one, and this ship once sailed on top of the sea rather than within it."

"What happened?" asked Tetra.

"The kraken attacked this ship, and devoured all of my crew, leaving me to watch my own body rot in the captain's cabin. At first, it can be a little overwhelming, watching crabs scuttle off with chunks of your own flesh. But then the starfish creep through the door and you realise how low on the food chain you've become."

"So, why do you need this ship if you're already dead?" Tetra asked and shrugged. "Seems I have a better use for it."

"*Gah!*" the Captain exclaimed. "I still believe there's a chance I can get out of here. Besides, the kraken lives and could easily return to take the rest of this ship. We must rebuild and sail far from here."

"Fine, fine," said Tetra. "Here's the wheel, attach it to your ship and let's go."

"Oh, you didn't think this ship needed just a wheel, did you?" replied the captain. "Look around you, it wouldn't outpace a dinghy rowed by a sponge and a starfish."

Captain Neureus moved across the deck towards one of the masts. There, he pointed at the ripped and tattered sails which hung like baggy trousers on an upside-down mannequin.

"And where am I supposed to get new sails?"

Tetra sighed, rolling her eyes further backwards than they usually were. Captain Neureus pointed south-east towards a wide-open area, where there was little to see and seemingly little to find.

"The fields of seagrass," said the Captain. "Lots of strange stuff seems to wash up there, I've even heard stories of other shipwrecks. Not quite like this one, mind you, but you might find what I… what we need there."

"Excuse me, Mr Captwain Nerwo, is it?" stuttered Tantalus, lifting his flipper up like he was addressing a teacher or someone of authority.

"Neureus, my shelled friend," said the captain, turning his head towards the turtle and raising his eyebrow.

"Neurweus, Neurweus," stuttered Tantalus, regaining his composure soon after his flipper fell back beside his hip. "Isn't the seagwass the home of some quite fewocious-looking sharks?"

Captain Neureus smiled at the turtle and shifted a glanced quickly at Tetra, who was hovered patiently by the side of the ship. Then he turned his back and began walking up the stairs clutching the wheel in both his hands. When he reached the top, he turned around and stared at both Tetra and Tantalus and gave another wry smile.

"Sharks are the least of your worries in this sea," the captain said in a hoarsely deep voice. "I suggest you leave when the sun rises. Predators usually prefer to hunt at night."

Tetra and Tantalus lay on the deck, using the tattered sails as both blankets and a weight to stop the windy currents carrying them off as they slept. The sky above their eyes felt empty and, if not for the moon and stars, there would have been nothing between it and the surface. Beneath the surface though, small fish, no bigger than Tetra's little finger, rose above the ship in their thousands. They moved as one, like a cloud dancing across the sky, changing shape at their own whim.

"That one looks like a giant jellyfwish," said Tantalus, pointing his flipper towards the school of fish.

"It seems like you only ever see jellyfish," said Tetra, giggling.

"Well, you can't blame me," chuckled Tantalus. "Some of the gweatest stories in life come stwaight from the belly."

"Now it looks like a large seagull," said Tetra, pointing towards the fish. "Kinda reminds of home."

"What is it like where you call home?" asked Tantalus.

"I always found it boring," said Tetra. "The same people, the same school, the same grandma with her silly stories. But now I kinda miss boring, especially my mum."

Tantalus smiled and looked up towards the school of fish that now took the shape of a turtle.

"Turtwles never get to meet their mums," said Tantalus.

"You don't?" said Tetra. "Why not?"

"We hatch from an egg on a beach," replied Tantalus. "From there, we wun to the sea before the seagulls can get us. Even the cwabs can snag you if you're not quick enough."

The fish changed from a turtle to what looked like a human with a long tail and two fins. The shape rode with the current and, as it breezed through like a gentle wind, the tail fluttered like that of a dolphin's. "A mermaid," said Tetra, pointing once more to the fish. Soon after, the fish quietly disappeared back into the darkest of the depths, where even the sunlight struggled to go, let alone the moonlight. By then, Tetra and Tantalus had fallen asleep. And when the first light hit the deck, they set off wandering through the fields of grass, the words of Captain Neureus planted in Tetra's mind –

they would be best to return to the ship before the last light.

Chapter 9
Shallow Skies

Before the sun could chase the moon away, Tetra and Tantalus were already surrounded by fields of sage green and large starfish awaiting their morning sunbathe. There were no shadows here, and if there were secrets, they had no refuge to hide. The grasslands were flat, with sand sprinkled between every blade and every growth. Small flowers bloomed in patches, usually purple with a white edging although red and yellow were not uncommon.

"You know, I never reawised how dewicious flowers are," said Tantalus, chomping his way through the seagrass. "These wed ones are particularly dewightful, did you want to twy some?"

"No, thanks," said Tetra, screwing her nose up. "We need to get out of these fields before the sharks show up. You heard the captain, right? We need to get back before it's dark."

"There's no harm in enjoying yourself while you're here," said Tantalus. "For someone that seeks adventure, you sure do avoid adventure."

"I don't see anything fun about sharks," replied Tetra. "Especially after my ordeal with the hydra back in the forest."

"Oooo…" said Tantalus, as he wandered away from Tetra with his tongue hanging out of his mouth.

"Where are you going now?" asked Tetra, frowning as she gazed towards the distracted turtle.

"Don't mind me," said Tantalus. "I've just never tasted a bwue fwower before. I'm sure it'll twickle my tastebuds."

Tetra rolled her eyes and followed Tantalus, her arms brushing the tips of the seagrass as she slowly kicked her legs.

The blue flowers were different to the other flowers. While the purples, the reds and the yellows all had leafy petals with a white, bulbous centre, the blue flowers had bulky tentacles curving out in the shape of a cup. Tetra noticed how they moved slightly, not with the blow of the current or the drift of the tide, but at their own free will.

"I don't think these are flowers, Tantalus," said Tetra, gazing around at each blue flower as they pulsated like a snail slithering up a stem.

"Don't be silly," said Tantalus, scoffing his mouth with as many blue flowers as he could fit in. "These flowers are dewicious. They have a jellyfwish quality to them, although much more slimy and fulling. Quite the snack."

As Tantalus munched, Tetra noticed one that dangled from his mouth. It squirmed, and when Tantalus chewed, it wiggled. And when it wiggled, it squirmed even more. Attached to the flower was a chunky, slimy body that was as white as the sands back home on the island. It had two eyes, both perched on top of a stalk, and when Tantalus chewed they bulged out as if they wanted to pop.

"Those aren't flowers," yelled Tetra. "They look like slugs!"

"Swugs," mumbled Tantalus, with blue flowers stuffed in his mouth. "But they're dewicious."

"That's disgusting," said Tetra, screwing up her nose and her mouth almost sinking lower than her neck.

It wasn't long before the patch of blue was turned into a patch of green. Where the slugs once roamed they no longer roamed, now sitting quietly in Tantalus' belly instead. There were other blue patches, but Tetra made sure to avoid them, as a hungry turtle would delay her finding the sails and further risk being in the fields before nightfall.

"My belly doesn't feel so good," moaned Tantalus, clutching his belly with his flippers.

"I am not surprised," said Tetra, with a wry grin on her face. "Those slugs were probably poisonous."

"Dewicious can't be poisonous," said Tantalus. "I sure wish turtwles could throw up right now though."

"Turtles can't throw up?" questioned Tetra, raising her eyebrow.

"Nope," chuckled Tantalus. "Once the dewicious is in, there's only one way it's coming out and it isn't always pretty." Before Tantalus could explain anymore, a strange shadow stumbled above them. Not long after, another stumbled past, and then another, before a whole flock of shadows were stumbling past them at a gentle speed.

"Lay low," said Tantalus, as he pulled Tetra down amongst the seagrass. They watched from below as giant jellybeasts swarmed close to the surface. Oddly, the jellybeasts seemed a little different to the usual. They were still huge, and they were still jelly, only their shape resembled more of a plastic bag than it did a jellyfish. Their tentacles, usually wildly independent, had now fused together on both sides, looking like a handle.

"I sure wish my belly didn't hurt," said Tantalus. "These jellyfwish look even more dewicious."

"You cannot be serious?" asked Tetra. "They look liked giant plastic bags."

"Pwastic bags or not, if I hadn't of eaten those swugs I for sure would be eating one of them jellyfwish right now," replied Tantalus.

"Don't you care what you eat?" asked Tetra, with her eyes shifted upwards watching the jelly beasts swim past in their hundreds.

"Oh, I care," said Tantalus. "As far as I'm concerned, there are three major food groups: dewicious, dewightful and dewectable."

"And which do plastic bags fall under?" asked Tetra.

"Well, if they're anything like the jellyfwish, both dewicious and dewightful," said Tantalus as he licked his lips.

The swarm of jellybeasts covered the surface for miles, all heading in one direction, past the grasslands and with the tide over the horizon, which was now a dark blue. The same direction Tetra and Tantalus were headed, where a subtle red lingered like the burning ashes of a great bonfire.

They began to paddle away from the swarm and snuck between each blade of grass and every petal of flower. As they drifted further away from the swarm, they slowly rose from the seabed, until the swarm was but a distant cloud stretching across the horizon. Where they were now, the grass was thinner and the sand was denser.

A small dinghy, barely big enough for one-person, lay half buried in the seabed. Its wooden body was rotten, its paddles mangled, and there was nothing but old fishing net inside its shell. Tetra sighed; there were no sails. But there was further debris that trailed towards the now crimson mist that haunted the edge of the horizon.

There was shrapnel, sharp enough to pierce the skin of a shark, and splotches of red sand that dripped sporadically across the sea floor. Pieces of torn net were also tangled in some of the grass, and where it tangled tight, the grass itself was no longer sage green but a chartreuse colour (no different to when the sun dries out the grass above the surface).

Tetra and Tantalus followed the junk, and as it happened, the junk followed them. As they swam above much of the debris, the current would bring more junk, some even swept past both Tetra and Tantalus as it bounced around the sand.

Further along, a wooden mast poked from under the seabed. Old rope dangled from the top, with lichen smothered all over its rough surface. Tetra began to dig around the mast, but it was an impossible task. The mast was so deeply buried that before Tetra could dig far enough, the sand would cascade down, refilling the hole. If there was a ship below the sand, its secrets were to be kept hidden.

A few paddles away, an old flag drifted silently above the seagrass. It was black, with a white skull in the centre, above two white sabre swords. It was torn, much like everything else that Tetra and Tantalus had encountered, with splotches of red staining parts of its fabric.

Beneath its shadow, a small piece of a larger net lay tangled, but moving, in the grass. Tetra swam closer, and the closer she swam towards the net, the more it moved.

"I think something might be trapped in there," said Tetra, turning to face Tantalus who was still hovering by the flag.

Tetra swam even closer to get a better look. and when she was within touching distance, she noticed a small tail, curled up like spring, sticking out from the knotted and twisted net. She picked up the net, and before she could get a could grip on it, the tail sprung straight and wriggled and wiggled until Tetra dropped it.

"I can't help you if you keep wiggling," said Tetra, picking up the net once more. She began to untie much of the rope, keeping a firmer grip on the net this time as the small creature continued to frenzy in her hands. After much struggle, several drops, and more than an ounce of frowns, the knots released, and a small creature danced out of the net.

Chapter 10
Graceful Encounters

In the classroom, on top of a dusty-looking cupboard next to the window, there had been a small glass bowl where a small goldfish lived. In between maths, science and boredom, Tetra often found herself staring into the bowl and watching the goldfish swim around and around in circles. It had a castle and some gravel, but everything else was merely walls and confinement, and it reminded Tetra of how she felt on the island.

While the small creature that Tetra had freed was pale blue instead of gold, had a long trumpet snout instead of a gormless, open mouth, and even a long, curly tail instead of short, petal-like fins, it felt remarkably similar to the goldfish at school. It circled around her, blowing bubbles into the sea, many of which popped into Tetra's face. And when Tetra spoke, it did not reply, instead it played charades with its tail and its small, delicate fins.

"Seahorses, always the quiet critters," said Tantalus. "This one looks like a baby, we should find its father and be on our way."

"A baby?" said Tetra. "I thought all seahorses were about this size."

"Not awound here," chuckled Tantalus. "Many can gwow bigger than me, and that's before they've had dinner."

"She sure likes to blow bubbles," said Tetra. "Let's call her Bubbles."

"Bubbles?" said Tantalus, munching on a flower in the

seagrass. "She's your seahorse now."

"How can she be mine?" asked Tetra. "I've never even seen a horse before, let alone look after a seahorse. There must be other seahorse around here."

They carried on following the trail of debris, and the further they swam, the more drops of red stained the sand. The seagrass was slowly becoming patchy. Gone were the magnificent fields of purple flowers and blue sea slugs, replaced by a reddening sand and brown stalks that crumbled to the touch.

The sea itself began to take on a crimson hue, with its usual taste of salt becoming slightly metallic. Even Tantalus, with his odd tastes, showed his displeasure at the red mist slowly seeping through much of the underwater savannah.

"There has to be a sail somewhere in this junk," said Tetra, with more lines across her forehead than her grandmother. Bubbles whizzed around, leaving a trail of bubbles wherever she went, sliding through all the places Tetra couldn't reach.

"Well, at least someone is helping, unlike that lazy turtle," said Tetra, indicating Tantalus swimming slowly, upside down with his front flippers on his belly.

"What's the hurry?" Tantalus said. "The sun is out, I have a full belly of flowers and the junk is going nowhere. Besides, I can't concentwate with this weird, red mist sliding up my nostwils."

"We need to find the sails before nightfall," Tetra said sternly, with Bubbles floating above her shoulder, making a squeak out of her trumpet.

"Can't we just have a small midday nap?" yawned Tantalus. "I can taste the jellyfwish in my dweams."

"Come on, Bubbles, we will find the sails on or own," said Tetra, turning around and rummaging through the junk as Bubbles followed close behind.

"Wouldn't it have been easier to just wepair the sails on the ship?" said Tantalus, still drifting upside down.

"How?" said Tetra, turning around to face the turtle once more.

"I don't know," said Tantalus. "I just don't twust a ghost who keeps his own skeleton in a wittle cabin, who then sends us out here in search of some sails in wed water."

Bubbles looked at Tetra, then looked back at Tantalus, then looked back at Tetra, before hiding behind Tetra's shoulder. Tetra's eyes honed in on Tantalus like thunder from the sky raging down onto the ground. There was a pause, a silence, a few seconds where the sound of the grass was the loudest noise around.

"Captain Neureus is my only way out of here," Tetra said quietly, holding in the urge to yell. "We need to find these sails before night time."

"Well, OK," Tantalus sighed, rolling back over. "But wherever he's going to take us, there better be more jellyfwish than my belly can handle." His belly gurgled a strange noise, and continued to gurgle for longer than any belly had ever gurgled. He patted it and smiled.

After following the trail of debris further, Bubbles' usual excitement was becoming less frequent, and the bubbles from her trumpet had all but ended. Rather than dancing and frolicking around Tetra, she started to move erratically and darted off in another direction. Tetra and Tantalus pursued the young seahorse, leading them to another small boat half buried into the seabed.

Inside, there were rusted harpoons, longer than the boat itself, and nets, filled with fish bones and some unidentifiable carcasses. Not far from the wreckage, Bubbles could be seen lying on the ground next to a large net. Caught in the net was a large seahorse, bigger than Tantalus with giant blue fins stretching down its back like a mane. It was lying motionless.

The net around the large seahorse had cut into his skin, with much of the rope wrapping around his neck and torso. His trumpet played no bubbles, nor a melody of droplets, but a sullen emptiness of silence. It was inside the net that a magnificent stead had stopped his gallop and it was there where he would lay for an eternity.

"Well, I think we know what happened to her father," whispered Tantalus.

Tetra didn't say a word, nor did she really know how to move. If there were tears, they washed away like scarlet diamonds falling to the ground. Tetra's father had disappeared long before, and she assumed he had died at sea, at least that's what her grandmother used to say. But this felt different.

"Quite unsettling, isn't it?" said Tantalus.

"What should I do?" asked Tetra.

"Nothing you can do weally," said Tantalus. "Sometimes just waiting is all there is to do… especially when your belly wumbles and there's nothing to eat."

Tetra drifted towards Bubbles and sat down next to her, holding onto a nearby rock as the current breezed through her hair. The red mist was deepening, the sun was falling and the captain's words for now had been forgotten. The little seahorse, with its tail curled up holding the net, sunk her head into the sand.

In the distance, four shadows approached from the east. As they moved closer, the four shadows became five, and then six and then maybe eleven. Soon, more than a dozen large shadows were swimming towards the wreckage. In the open grasslands, there could be nowhere to hide.

"Looks like your luck didn't dwy out just yet," Tantalus said, with a smile beaming across his wrinkly face.

"What do you mean?" asked Tetra.

"You said you needed to find a herd of seahorses and here comes a large one wight now."

Tetra looked at Bubbles and she felt a sudden wrench from her chest that she hadn't felt before. It wasn't guilt, nor was it entirely sadness, but more a realisation that the Bubbles she had just met was soon to leave her.

One seahorse approached Tetra, and with a nod, turned to Bubbles and gave her a small nudge. When the nudge didn't awaken the young seahorse, the older seahorse tried another nudge, and then another until Bubbles opened her eyes.

Soon Bubbles was back on her feet, dancing and trumpeting like she had done before. But then she looked back at the dead body lying tangled and sadness filled her eyes once more. All the seahorses gathered around, gently pushing Tetra out of the ring, leaving her watching on the side-lines.

"Well, that's a little rude," Tetra mumbled.

"It seems your Bubbles has found her herd," said Tantalus.

"Yeah..." Tetra sighed, gazing as the herd raised their heads and hooted towards the moonlit sky. "Come on, Tantalus, we must keep moving. We have a sail to find."

Tetra and Tantalus moved towards the red horizon, a deepening rouge that blushed across the sand. As they moved away, streams of bubbles appeared around them, more frequently than ever before. Then, there, right behind them was Bubbles herself, whizzing around Tetra in a whirlpool of ardour.

"You need to leave with your herd now," said Tetra, pushing the young seahorse away.

The bubbles stopped and the dancing ceased, and the young seahorse's head fell towards the sand as she hovered motionless.

"We will meet again," said Tetra, raising her head towards Bubbles. The young seahorse looked up, and danced again, blowing bubbles high into the sea. Then they hugged and moved in separate directions, the herd towards the blue, Tetra and Tantalus towards the red.

Chapter 11
Crimson Mist

The crimson mist blinded Tetra's eyes. She could hear Tantalus paddling, she could feel the small waves that he made, but she couldn't see a flipper or a shell behind her. The sand below was just that. When her hands glided across the seafloor, there wasn't a blade of grass, nor petal or a slug, but sand and dust that thickened the red mist when disturbed.

"Are you still there?" asked Tetra, looking behind her to see if she could see the big turtle.

"Just about," a chuckle close behind said. "Although, I can only just about see your feet paddlwing in fwont."

"How are we supposed to find a sail in this mist?" asked Tetra.

"I'm not entirely sure what it is," said Tantalus. "But it sure doesn't fill me with much confwidence."

"We have to keep going," said Tetra. "It's already dark and we haven't found the sail yet. The captain said we should get back before dark!"

"Well, with any wuck, if we can't see the sharks, they can't see us," laughed Tantalus.

They travelled deeper into the mist, and the more rouge it became, the harder it was to see. Even Tetra's movements felt heavy, like the sea had become as thick as custard and her body as heavy as an anchor. Fortunately, there was no further to sink as the seabed was already inches from her belly, and the water was shallow in this part of the sea.

Occasionally, Tetra's hands would find something on the seafloor, usually an old, rusted bolt or netting that was slimy to the touch. Regardless, everything that was there, shouldn't have been there, even if it had been there longer than Tantalus had existed.

As they travelled through the murk and the fog, Tetra noticed a piece of fabric moving in a circle. It rolled at first, and then it bounced and ricocheted between loose stones (which themselves soon started rolling in circles too). Then the bolts and the other metallic items on the seafloor were swirling too around Tetra and Tantalus.

Once the rubbish had risen, it didn't seem to want to go down, swirling higher and higher into the sea. Then Tetra felt herself losing control as she was swept along, moving slowly in a circle around Tantalus. She felt nauseous, and the crimson mist that had once felt heavy now felt light as she began whirling higher and higher.

"Tantalus, help me!" she screamed, as she held her hand out towards him.

Tantalus raised his flipper towards her hand, but before she could grab it, he had started whirling too. Within a blink of an eye, they were both swirling around in a tornado of filth and red fog.

"I shouldn't have eaten those bwue flowers," said Tantalus, as bluish brown sludge evacuated the back end of him and into the tornado, swirling its way around hitting Tetra and everything else within it.

"I hope you're joking," squealed Tetra, unable to wipe the sludge off her face as the force of the tornado became too great.

"I'm so-so-so sorry," stuttered Tantalus, as more sludge left his body. "I don't think it's gonna stop."

"Please hold it in!" squealed Tetra.

"I ca-ca can't," he whimpered. "My bottom is on fire."

Soon the tornado was a tornado that not only moved quickly but smelled worse than a rotting whale. And rotten it was. The junk mixed with whatever had come out of Tantalus was an incredible concoction of tremendous stinks. With the crimson mist, the tornado became a vibrant purple of destructive odour.

Closer to the surface, the mist wasn't as dense. Whether that was the tornado or the heaviness of the mist, Tetra could not be certain. In the distance, Tetra could see other tornadoes whizzing around the desert of the sea. Trapped in their storms was mostly the same junk that Tetra and Tantalus had already found themselves swimming with.

"They're almost like whirlpools," Tetra jittered, as she continued to whizz around the tor-nado. "Although, whirlpools go down while these go up like tornadoes."

Tantalus didn't seem to be listening. His face looked like he had more blue sludge to eject. His flippers were firmly placed on his belly and his eyes were half closed as they spun around more and more.

"Please, no more," warned Tetra, "I don't need—" Before she could finish her words, the tornado began to slow down, and as it did, the rubbish began to fall back down to the seabed. Tetra and Tantalus remained near the surface; his face as green as it ever had been before. Before Tetra could say another word, she heaved, and as she heaved, she gagged. After one more gag, her own green sludge flew out in all directions.

"This is the last time you eat slugs," sulked Tetra, wiping her vomit from her lips. "That was the most disgusting thing that has ever happened to me."

"Do you see that over there?" Tantalus said, pointing his flipper towards a tornado. "It's the sail you were looking for!"

Tetra turned around and faced to where Tantalus was pointing. There, not too far from where they were, a sail was swirling around at the top of one of the weird underwater tornadoes. Her eyes lit up much like Tantalus' had, and without another murmur about the blue sludge, she grabbed his flipper and they swam towards the sail.

By the time they got to the sail, the tornado had descended and it was laying on the seabed. Where the red mist was coming from was now apparent. Whatever the red mist was, it was leaking from the sails that were wrapped up like a sausage roll.

"What do you think is hiding under the sail?" Tetra asked Tantalus.

"I'm afwaid to find out," Tantalus replied.

"I think we've been through worse so far," said Tetra. "I seem to be surviving everything at the moment. I guess this is what a real adventure is supposed to be. Surviving against all smells and disgusting problems."

"Maybe," Tantalus said after a brief pause. "But there are only so many times my shell can be scwaped before it quacks."

"Quacks," smirked Tetra. "Your shell is a duck?"

"Very funny," said the turtle. "I have twouble with certain words."

"I'm sorry, I'm sorry," said Tetra. "That was mean of me."

"That's alwight," chuckled Tantalus. "I did cause quite the stwink."

They both giggled as they approached the sail, ready to see what lay inside.

"I guess we should unravel the mystery," replied Tantalus.

They began to pull the sail, and as it rolled down, more red mist leaked out, blanketing their vision once more. Soon, the mist became a thick cloud, like a raincloud but a bludgeoning maroon. So deep was its colour that when it tried to rise towards the surface, it sunk even quicker, painting the dusty sand with the ominous crimson tinge.

The red mist was slow to fade, and even when it looked like it was about to subside, its crimson flow spilled out to paint the sea with an ever-deepening rouge. It was a painting like no other, like a brush wiping the canvas with nothing more than different shades of red and sometimes a quietly unnerving maroon.

When the mist had bled, and no more of the water could be fed, it started to leave slowly into the surrounding sea. The sand was still red, and the sails were a silent shade of pink, but underneath the mist was something unexpected

Rows of sharp teeth, like ivory daggers, flared from beneath the mist. There were many, hundreds even, in a mouth big enough to swallow Tantalus whole. The teeth they didn't snap though, nor did they snarl, but hung silently from the gums. They looked sharp enough to pierce Tantalus' shell, and if given the chance, maybe they would. But something felt wrong.

As the fog gradually cleared, the owner of the teeth appeared. A dark grey, slender body, about as long as two buses parked in a row. Its eyes were as dark as a starless sky, looking banished of life, sending chills down Tetra's spine.

"I have a bad feeling about this shark," Tetra said, taking a closer look into its eyes.

"What do you mean?" Tantalus said. "This shark isn't going anywhere, its fins are missing."

"They are?" questioned Tetra, swimming around to take a closer look at the shark's back. "Oh, yes." She peered closer. "It looks like they were cut off."

"Better than it being awive, I suppose," Tantalus chuckled, tapping his flipper against the shark's body. "Imagine twying to escape this beast out in the open sea."

"I guess you're right," said Tetra. "But I can't help but feel a little bad for it."

"Do you think a shark would feel bad for you as it gnaws on your bones?" asked Tantalus, mimicking how a shark snapped its teeth. "Put yourself in my fwippers, I was bit by a shark and was wucky to live to tell the tale." He held up his flipper to show a small circular scar, no bigger than a bottle cap.

"Lucky to live the tale, huh?" Tetra laughed. "Looks more like you were bitten by a goldfish."

"I will have you know even small sharks can be dangerous," said Tantalus.

They grabbed the sail, Tetra lifting on one end and Tantalus biting on the other. They had begun to swim away from the shark when a grumbling noise came from behind. Tetra looked around to see the shark facing them.

Chapter 12
Hide and Teeth

Sharks used to swim by her island when the tide was right. A dorsal fin above the surface made all the swimmers and surfers dash for the safety of the beach. No one Tetra knew had ever died from a shark attack though, and only one had ever been bitten. Indeed, the hammerhead swarms in the summer attracted a lot of tourists. But this shark at the bottom of the sea, even without its fins, was perhaps the scariest she had ever seen before, and even bigger than she had ever imagined the biggest shark could ever be.

The shark stared back at her. It was motionless but sent a shiver down Tetra's spine. The scars where its fins had once been leaked the red mist, clouding the sea in a red haze that lingered heavily across the desert of the ocean floor.

"I think this is the part where we swim fast," whispered Tantalus.

"How do you out-swim a shark?" asked Tetra.

"It has no fins," whispered Tantalus.

They slowly backed away, still clutching onto the sails. Every inch mattered; the further they made it away from the shark, the more confident they felt that they could get back to the ship unscathed. It remained harrowing though, and time ticked slower than a clock in a crocodile's throat. Tetra kept an eye looking towards the horizon, and the other looked back towards the finless shark.

The water became clearer the further away from the shark they went. The red mist was fading, and the seabed below their feet was becoming less tinged. Indeed, the wreckages of boats were now more visible, as was a lot of netting that came with them.

They paddled steadily until the shark behind them was but a distant shadow and then, without much hesitation, they started to paddle harder until the shadow was nothing more than a speck on the horizon. Tetra sighed with relief, and Tantalus sighed back. They carried on past the desert until sprouts of grass started appearing once more.

"Maybe we should west our fwippers for a little bit," slurred Tantalus, with the sail still in his mouth. "At least for a few moments so I can have a small snack."

"Nope," replied Tetra. "That was only one dead shark, there might be hundreds around here. We need to get back to the ship."

"You know, the best jellyfwish come out at night," said Tantalus.

"So do the biggest sharks," replied Tetra.

There was a murmur behind them, like a splash, but quiet. Tetra and Tantalus looked back, but there was nothing but the open sea, and a bleak red on the horizon. Tetra carried on paddling forward, wanting to get back to the ship as soon as possible. Just seeing the purple flowers of the grasslands once more would give her some relief.

But, as it happened, the red on the horizon was growing larger once more. Soon, the red mist that once blocked their eyes was once again seeping around their bodies. Even the sand was suffering from its gory hue.

An upturned boat lay across the sand. It was larger than most of the wreckages Tetra had seen in the desert and large enough for both her and Tantalus. She moved closer to it, dropping the sail as she drifted. As her side of the sail sunk towards the sand, Tantalus opened his mouth and the rest thudded onto the floor.

"I have a bad feeling about the red mist," Tetra said. "We should hide for a little bit. Help me lift this old boat."

Tetra grabbed one end, and Tantalus the other ends, and they lifted the boat gently up. The red mist was coming in strong, and they didn't need to think twice about hiding underneath it. There was a small crack in the side through which Tetra could see out. The red mist was gathering fast, and soon all she could see was the fire of the mist circling around the boat.

"Looks like we're here for a while," Tetra said. "I don't think I can sleep though." She turned around to see the large turtle already comfortably snoozing in a small hole he had dug out beneath his body. She sighed and sat her back against the side of the boat and waited for the sun to rise.

Unfortunately, it would be a long wait for the sun to appear. While Tantalus snored into his dreams, Tetra couldn't stop peering through the gap in the boat. She could only see red and the occasional flicker of the sail. Even the sea was silent, at least most of the time. It sometimes fluttered, but nothing more than a gentle whisper across the great plain.

That wouldn't last though.

A stream flowed into a river, and a river into the sea. Small creatures flocked together and became a larger creature. A small flutter grew by the second, like a hurricane winding its way across the ocean or an avalanche bundling its way down a mountain. The red mist had begun moving erratically. Its flutters were now ferocious swipes that moved elegantly stalking its prey.

Tetra turned to look at Tantalus, but he was fast asleep, snoring away still like the hurricane outside was merely a whistle in the wind. Even a gentle nudge didn't wake him, only causing him to snort and murmur, and fidget in his hole.

"Wake up," Tetra whispered. "I think the shark is here."

Tantalus stirred, but didn't awaken. He flipped his flippers, chomped his teeth, and snored gently into his humble hole. Tetra tried nudging him all the more, but the more she nudged, the more he snored, and the more he snored, the more intense the red mist became.

Tetra peered through the gap in the boat once more. There was only darkness, a gloomy recluse that offered even less than the red mist had. She looked up, and to her surprise, the same rows and rows of sharp daggers lay hanging like icicles on a frozen cave's door. For the first time, the water felt cold. She sat back down and shivered, turning to Tantalus in hope that if left undisturbed, he won't snore so loudly.

But such was fate, a small crab was crawling along Tantalus' belly. And, to Tetra's horror, it was tickling Tantalus into quiet, sleepy giggles. Soon he was fidgeting, and when he fidgeted, so did the boat. And when the boat rocked, the red mist thickened, and the teeth began to poke through the gap.

The small crab had by now crawled along his belly and onto one of his flippers. The giggling soon stopped, and Tantalus began to flail, all the while still asleep. Tetra tried to hold him back but she was too small to control a sleeping turtle, especially one with a crab crawling up his flipper.

Within a blink of an eye, everything stopped. Tantalus fell silent, the red mist dropped, and the crab stood dormant. The crab squeezed its pincer firmly on Tantalus' flipper and at that moment, his eyes spring wide open.

"Ouch!" he yelled at the top of his voice, his head banging against the boat, causing it to shake.

"Uhoh," Tetra murmured, her eyes fixed on the gap in the boat.

"Crabs are a pain in the fwipper," Tantalus whinged to himself, flicking away the crab. "What's wrong, Tewra?"

Tetra stayed silent, staring into the gap and, just then, the boat was hurled off them and a large finless shark faced them, staring into their eyes. Its eyes, still as dark as before, had new life sparkling into them. Its teeth hung like rows of daggers, each dripping with a crimson mist.

"So, it was you two who stole my bandage!" the shark bellowed.

Tetra and Tantalus said nothing, just stared into the beast's eyes as it gazed into theirs. The red mist flowed from its scars, and as it flowed, it wept into the sand like tears dripping onto the floor.

Tetra slowly rose to be face to face with the shark. Her hands were shaking and her feet trembling, but her eyes fixed on the great beast. It looked even bigger than before, certainly big enough to swallow her and Tantalus whole. But she had survived this long in the sea, and she wasn't about to give up just yet.

Chapter 13
In the Jaws of Defeat

The shark's pupils dilated as it honed its gaze directly into Tetra's eyes. Her snout began to twitch, and as it twitched, her mouth opened wider, showing chunks of flesh dangling from her gums. Soon, the shark was gagging.

"What's that smell?" the shark growled. "Smells like the dung of a rotting whale carcass."

Tantalus shied away, hiding behind Tetra, but the turtle was so massive and Tetra was so small, it didn't have the desired effect.

"I ate a bad swug," the turtle murmured.

"You eat slugs!" the shark bellowed. "That's filthy. The odour going up my nose is making me even more angry!"

"What do you want?" Tetra asked the shark.

"What you stole," said the shark. "Plus a snack on the side."

"I need the sail," replied Tetra.

"Oh, you think your ship is more important than my life?" replied the shark, edging slowly closer towards Tetra.

"I didn't say that," said Tetra.

"But you implied it," said the shark. "I see we have another human, perhaps posing as a mermaid but not fooling anyone with those feet for fins, thinking they can just take whatever they find in the ocean, then even leaving the place in a right stink."

"That isn't true!" yelled Tetra. "I didn't ask to be down here."

"I didn't ask you to be here either," growled the shark. It was then that the shark began to widen her jaws, flashing her gums and rolling her eyes back within her head. Within a split second, the jaws came crashing down above Tetra's head, and a tumbling turtle was swooping and zooming away from the shark with Tetra on his back.

"Time to fwy or be dinner," Tantalus stuttered while catching his breath.

"We can't leave the sail!" said Tetra, looking back towards it, as it lay by the upturned boat, flickering in the current.

"We can come back for it," Tantalus stuttered. "I'm not weady for my shell to be a bowl."

Tantalus flew into the sea, his flipper scraping against the surface as he made sharp turns to weave around the desert. He zoomed between the wreckages of boats and pushed his body through chains and floating planks of wood, as Tetra held on to his shell for dear life.

Behind them, a finless shark, with red running from her scars, was chasing in pursuit. Where Tantalus had to weave, she could crash through, and what Tantalus had to avoid, she could smash into two. A boat drifting along the seabed could only shatter faced with the sheer size of her body, and the nylon nets that stalked and captured so many fish could only tear when her snout crashed through them.

Tantalus was fast, but the shark was faster. Every obstacle in his way only allowed the shark to get an inch closer. Soon, she was snapping at his flippers, and he could only use his smaller frame to make sharp turns away from the enormous jaws.

"You need to swim faster!" yelled Tetra, looking behind at the shark's dark void of a mouth.

"I am twying," Tantalus panted. "But my fwippers are weady to collapse."

Ahead, more netting lay tangled on the seabed, riddled with the corpses of unfortunate fish. There was also a wire underneath the netting that led towards a wreckage of a small ship. Tantalus sharply swam towards the surface, his belly facing the netting as he glided upwards. The shark crashed straight through the netting, with much of it trapped between her teeth as she shook her head from side to side.

"Head towards that small ship," said Tetra, pointing towards it.

Tantalus surged towards it, ignoring the shark as she became enraged by the netting in her teeth. The ship was unlike the other wreckage. Instead of a wooden exterior, it was made from metal, most likely steel. It didn't have sails, nor did it have oars, but had a great propellor at its rear that would have once pushed it across the ocean surface.

On its deck, the metal wire was hooked up to a lever, and could be wound up like a hosepipe. Where the wire stopped, the sand was slightly disturbed and raised above the rest of the seabed by about an inch. The shark, still fighting the netting caught between her teeth, raged ferociously above the dishevelled sand.

"There's something underneath the sand," said Tetra. "Something big. Help me pull this lever."

Tantalus looked at her confused, glancing one look at the lever, then another at the sand, then an even closer look at the outstretched wire.

"Come on!" Tetra urged. "We don't have long before the shark comes back for us."

Tantalus lent his flipper and they both began to tug down on the lever. It was stiff, and when it moved, it jolted and clunked. And after three clunks, several jolts, and some tired Tetra arms, the wire slowly began to wind and coil around.

The dishevelled sand started to tumble like a waterfall, and as the sand tumbled and dispersed into the sea, clouds of dust formed around the shark. There were waves within the dust cloud, like something inside was angry and ferociously scrambling around. The plumes of sand soon reached the ship and both Tetra and Tantalus began to cough while continuing to pull on the lever.

As the dust settled, a huge iron net appeared from where the cloud had been. Inside the net, an angry shark thrashed around, replacing a cloud of sand with a cloud of morbid red. Her teeth gnawed at the metal, but alas, not even teeth as sharp as daggers could break the chainmail on this net.

Tetra and Tantalus approached the net slowly, their eyes fixed on the great beast that not so long before had been chasing them with a great appetite. They hovered beneath her shadow and watched as she struggled, bleeding more red plumes than she had before.

"I suppose this is what you wanted?" growled the shark.

"Not really," replied Tetra. "But you left me no choice."

"You don't belong here," replied the shark. "No human belongs here. The ocean belongs to me."

"Well, not anymore," replied Tetra, dusting her hands. "Let's go, Tantalus, I think we left the sail this way."

"You won't escape the sea," the shark growled as Tetra and Tantalus moved. "Your fate is already sealed."

****

Tetra and Tantalus retraced their paddles. Through much of the underwater desert, past all the wreckages and the disgusting junk, until they reached the upside-down boat. Next to it, lying patiently amongst the sand, the pink-drenched sail awaited.

"What do you think happened to that shark back there?" Tetra asked Tantalus.

"Well, it's twapped in a metal net," chuckled Tantalus.

"No, I mean her fins," said Tetra. "What happened to her fins?"

"*Hmm,*" Tantalus hummed, with his flipper rubbing his chin. "I once saw an octopus without all his wegs, but he wouldn't say much about it. He did hide when shadows appeared from above though."

"I just find it sad," said Tetra. "Maybe she wouldn't be so angry if she still had her fins."

"No, but she would still be hungwy," said Tantalus.

As the sun kissed the surface of the ocean, the red mist began to fade. The growls grew silent, and when they stopped, the water became clear once more and the grasslands could be seen in the distance.

They waded through, above the purple flowers and beyond the blue slugs, until on the horizon they could see the captain's ship: the one that neither sunk nor floated. It glimmered below the sun, dazzled almost, and even its ripped sails felt like a ray of hope after their ordeal with the shark. They swam forward slowly, carrying the sail steadily, until they were just beneath the old ship.

"I never thought I'd miss this ship," Tetra said.

"Something looks a wittle different this time," said Tantalus.

"Yeah, I know," said Tetra. "Maybe it's almost ready to go, Captain Neureus just needs this sail, and we can sail on home."

They landed onto the deck and dropped the sails on the floor. The ship though was more different than Tetra could had ever expected. They were not alone. There were now at least twenty other ghosts, all grimacing as much as the next one. Ghouls of ancient sailors, maybe even the spirits of pirates, all marauding across the deck. And above on the wheel, a familiar sight, a Captain Neureus proudly standing, glancing down at Tetra and the turtle.

"I see you were most successful," said the captain. "Come to my cabin, let us reminisce about what lies ahead."

The captain vanished like an octopus though a crack. The other sailors stared at Tetra, and as they stared, the few fangs they had left in their mouths began to smile. Soon, a smile turned to a raucous laughter, and the moment of joy Tetra and Tantalus had just felt vanished.

"I see da wee girl found us breakfast," laughed one of the pirates, his ghostly eyes popping out of his ghostly head. Tetra could only imagine how deformed he must have been in life.

"Somehow, I don't feel like I'm going to be part of this cwew," whispered Tantalus.

"Relax," said Tetra. "The captain hasn't let me down yet."

"But has he done anything yet?" replied Tantalus.

"No," sighed Tetra. "But nothing is better than something bad."

"His skeleton was something bad," said Tantalus.

"This is still my only way out of here," said Tetra.

As they approached the cabin door, it opened by itself. Tetra turned to face the deck, and as she did, the laughter stopped, and the ghosts disappeared. She looked ahead and there, sat in the chair, was Captain Neureus waiting for them.

Chapter 14
A Captain without a Hat

In the far corner, a skeleton stood without an arm or a head. Its head sat on the captain's table, its face as vacant as it had been the last time Tetra encountered it. Much else lay undisturbed. That was until Tetra walked in and saw four gigantic skulls, each grimacing as much as the next, with large teeth and large snouts, sat side-by-side next to the globe.

"Fabulous, aren't they?" said the captain. "To think, they were once terrorising the forest."

"This was the hydra?" gasped Tetra, unable to look away from the three skulls. "How did you kill it?"

"This ol' ship has some life in it yet," said the captain, ignoring her question. "And with your help, and with your slightly bloodstained sails, she's certainly ready to sail back to your island."

"You mean it?" exclaimed Tetra. "I can go home now?"

"I didn't say that," said the captain. "But almost. As you might have noticed, I have my crew back. A fine crew they are, a little dim-witted maybe, but with my captainship they move this ship like there's a tornado in the sails."

The captain stood from his chair and picked up his skull. He looked into the holes where his eyes used to be, and then looked back at Tetra and smiled.

"Sometimes a crew needs to be reminded who the captain is," the captain said. "And sometimes, that is as easy as wearing a captain's hat. I lost mine east of here, somewhere around a coral reef..." He fell silent.

Tetra's eyebrow slowly raised until they were nearly as high as the top of her head. "You want me to put my life in danger once more... for a hat?" she asked.

"Trust me, your life would be in more danger on this ship without a captain," the captain said, drifting over towards her. "And a captain without a hat isn't really a captain at all."

Tetra turned to Tantalus. He was already looking back her, his lips visibly trembling. A commotion could be heard outside the cabin. Loud bangs and aggressive laughter knocked on the door like a hurricane battering the coastline. It was inescapable and made both Tetra and Tantalus shudder.

"You see," the captain said, placing his hand on Tetra's back, "without my hat, the idiots out there won't know what to do with themselves. You'll be walking the plank down into the largest trench this side of the ocean."

"But you only need to drop me off on my island and then you can be on your way," Tetra replied.

"I wish I could do that right now," said the captain, his ghoulish eyes brightening as he smiled at Tetra. "But without my hat, this crew won't even make it to the surface. We're a long way down and this ship can still sink a little further without the right guidance."

"Shall we just go, Tetwa," stuttered Tantalus, looking through a gap in the door. "Those piwates are looking at me with hungwy eyes."

"Pirates!" said the captain. "A pirate sails without law or code. No, we were more... privateers."

"Privateers?" replied Tetra. "I've heard about them, weren't they—"

"We could discuss my work in life all day," interrupted the captain. "But whether I'm a pirate, privateer or even maybe a buccaneer, truth be told, you won't be getting home without my ship."

Tetra glanced around the room. The skeleton and its ominous smile looked back, vacantly now, but alive in Tetra's mind. Even the hydra, perhaps more dead than the captain himself, still seemed to growl when Tetra looked at it. At least that's what she felt she heard.

"Come on, Tantalus," said Tetra, backing away from the captain. "Let's go get his hat."

Tantalus nudged the door back open and there stood in front of them was the captain's crew once more. They were still grinning.

Tetra and Tantalus slowly paddled down the steps and between the pirates. She looked to her left and one pirate, grinning like they all did, chuckling like they all did, even had the audacity to lick his lips at the sight of her.

Another put his hand on her shoulder and growled. His grip was cold, and her spine felt like an icicle ready to snap. She lowered her shoulder and pushed him away, but her hands fell through him like he was nothing but a whisper in the tide.

Beside her, Tantalus had his flippers over his mouth and was jittering. He seemed to be murmuring to himself that 'he wasn't a jellyfish', to which Tetra assumed he meant he wasn't dinner. But these were ghosts, they couldn't eat, surely? Where would the food go? Through their bodies and down to the seabed where a sneaky crab would crawl along and munch on it. Tetra remained unsure.

"Let our guests through," Captain Neureus said from behind them, standing above the stairs. "When they return, I want them to be treated…accordingly."

"See, he's not so bad," whispered Tetra towards Tantalus.

"I'm not so sure," jittered Tantalus. "They keep wicking their wips at me."

The pirates stepped back as the captain began to slowly walk down the steps, his eyes jerking around the ship. His finger slid against the rail, then he examined the dust on his finger and smiled.

"I think we can get this ship into better shape, don't you?" he growled towards his crew.

Tetra turned to see all the pirates dragging themselves back to work. Several of them began removing the shreds of old sails and within a few moments, they were off, and the new sails were on, the red mist still drenched all over it.

"I like it," said the captain, leaning back and admiring the new sail. "The red tinge really gives my ship a new edge. Do you see what I mean, Roger?"

"Yes, Captain," one of the crew muttered, presumably Roger.

"It gives it a..." The captain paused, with his hand on his chin. "An ambitious vibe. What do you say to that, Roger?"

"Yes, Captain," presumably Roger muttered once more.

Tetra turned around, unsure what to think. She got to the bow of the ship and stared out towards the east. It looked flat and empty, with only a tiny glimmer of white on the horizon. She turned to Tantalus and nodded, and they began to move forward.

"Oh, one last thing," said the captain, drifting towards her. "If you happen by a harpoon, bring it back too please. It would be most... advantageous in my... in our adventure."

"A harpoon?" questioned Tetra, raising her eyebrow.

"Consider it a spear of the sea," said the captain. "The sea is dangerous, after all. We wouldn't want to bump into any krakens on our way home, aye?"

"Oooo, calamawi!" said Tantalus, drooling from one side of his mouth.

"I think you'd be the calamari to the Kraken, turtle," snarled the captain, with a side-grin. Tantalus soon stopped drooling and tried to sink into his shell.

"No one is going to be calamari," said Tetra, waving her hands around. "Krakens do not exist. Now about this harpoon—"

"It's quite simple really," said the captain. "You either want to be alive at the end of this adventure or you don't. The harpoon aids us in our survival. You either fight the sea or you die within it. Think about it."

He moved away back towards the sails, giving them another close inspection. He patted Presumably Roger on his shoulder and carried on up his stairs and back to his cabin.

Tetra turned around, looking back towards the white glimmer on the horizon.

"Well, here goes another adventure, Tantalus," she whispered.

"And I hope it won't be my wast," he jittered.

They jetted off away from the ship, first staying close to the surface, before sliding back down towards the seabed to check out some crabs fighting over a can of beans.

"I sure hope we can get dinner along the way," said Tantalus. "My belly is wumbling!"

Chapter 15
Watch the Flippers!

The sea was warmer, not as hot as a bath, but there was enough heat for Tetra to feel the change on her skin. Beneath them, there was nothing more than static starfish and the occasional flatfish burying into the sand.

Small holes sporadically littered the seafloor. Every now and then, a bubble would leave one of the holes and rise until it burst on the surface. It was nothing spectacular, the bubbles were neither giant nor mysterious, but something about the holes from which they came was unappealing to Tetra.

"Have you ever heard about trypophobia?" Tetra asked Tantalus.

"Twy-po-what now?" replied Tantalus, his flipper rubbing against his chin.

"Trypophobia, it's the fear of holes," said Tetra, her eyes darting between each hole.

"You have a fear of holes?" asked Tantalus.

"I didn't used to, but now I do," replied Tetra.

"Some of my favouwite places to be in the sea are holes," chuckled Tantalus. "Did I ever tell you about jellyfwish cave?"

"No, but my guess is, it's a cave filled with jellyfish?" said Tetra, her eyebrow raised with smirk.

"It's a cave filled with jellyfwish," said Tantalus.

"Mind blowing," replied Tetra.

"And they're gweat places to hide fwom sharks," replied

Tantalus.

"Or a great place for an electric beast to sneak up on you," said Tetra.

Tantalus rested his flipper on his chin. He usually did that when he had to think about something Tetra had said, which only made Tetra smirk a little more. A small victory for her, even if Tantalus wasn't playing games.

"An electwic beast," he replied finally. "Never seen one of them. Did you say there was one back in the fowest?"

"Yes."

"Oh," replied Tantalus, flipping shell-side down again, with his flippers behind his head. "Doesn't seem like it would be in jellyfwish cave then."

"If there's one, there must be others," said Tetra.

"There's only one Tantawus," chuckled Tantalus.

"I guess you're right," muttered Tetra, keeping her eye on all the holes dotted around the floor.

The fish they passed seemed to be mostly avoiding the bubbles, and when a hole opened, they quickly scattered. They didn't have many places to scatter to though, for when they dispersed from one hole, several others would open underneath them. After a while, clouds of sand would kick up, and when the sand settled, some of the fish would disappear.

Tetra and Tantalus waded through slowly. As their shadows passed the holes, some would close up, only to open up again once they had gone. Tantalus' flippers occasionally scraped the seabed, brushing up sand and shells with it. He seemed oblivious, twirling around one minute, and then lying upside down the other.

The clouds of sand built up once more and Tantalus waded through without hesitation. Tetra paddled closely behind, a cold shiver sliding down her spine once more. The sea remained clear near the surface, but down by the seabed, everything was a little blurred.

"Ouch!" screamed Tantalus, as he flurried towards the surface, waving his flipper around.

"What is it?" yelled Tetra, following close behind but still unable to see too clearly.

"Look at my flipper," said Tantalus, raising his flipper to show a long, skinny creature, about a metre in length, biting down with huge mandibles. It had segments like a centipede, with sharp spikes that seemed better for anchoring it into the sand rather than swimming in the sea.

By now, all the fish had dispersed and were nowhere to be seen, perhaps afraid of this worm-like beast attached to Tantalus. It wiggled and wriggled, and the more Tantalus flapped his flipper, the deeper its mandibles sunk into his flesh.

"Ouch!" Tantalus screamed some more, zooming in a circle around Tetra.

"You need to stay still," yelled Tetra. "I can't help you if you keep moving."

"When did I become everything's dinner?" cried Tantalus, still frantically swimming around in a circle.

"Oh please, everything always seems to be your dinner," Tetra yelled back.

At that moment, something else caught Tetra's eye. While Tantalus continued his panic, Tetra spotted a small, dull light. It wasn't too far away, and it was coming their way.

As the light got brighter, despite the worm beast, Tantalus stopped panicking and gazed at it too. The worm beast still sinking its giant mandibles into his flipper.

"What is that?" asked Tantalus.

"I have no idea," said Tetra.

Soon the light was staring at them in the face and, just behind the light, were several huge teeth and white, blank eyes. Tetra was relieved that the rest of the creature wasn't quite so fearsome. Its teeth could barely fit in its mouth, and its body was no bigger than one of Tantalus' flippers.

"I don't suppose he bites too," whispered Tantalus in Tetra's ear.

"Don't be so rude," Tetra whispered back.

"This little light of mine," the creature sung. "I'm going to let it shine."

"The only thing worse than his teeth is his singing," Tantalus whispered to Tetra.

"Hello weary travellers," the creature said. "My name is Apollo. You wouldn't happen to know which way it is to the wossname... the forest?"

"It was south-west of here," said Tetra. "But it was burnt down by a hydra."

"Well, that's horribly unfortunate," said Apollo. "Everywhere I go, there seems to be some kind of wossname... disaster."

"Must be the singing," Tantalus whispered in Tetra's ear and she nudged him away.

"Did you happen to travel by a coral reef?" Tetra asked Apollo.

"Ah yes," said Apollo. "Not too far from here, although it wasn't what I expected, I must say. Oh my wossname friend," Apollo said to Tantalus. "There appears to be a worm attached to your flipper."

"Oh," said Tantalus, looking back at his flipper. He turned purple and then yelled ouch some more, whizzing around in a circle.

"Sorry," replied Apollo. "Where I'm from, we get creatures like this too... only much bigger. They don't like the light much. Here..."

Apollo approached Tantalus' flipper and without a second of hesitation, the light on his forehead grew brighter. And as the light grew, the mandibles from the worm beast slowly loosened. Soon, the light was so bright that Tetra couldn't see what was going on until it was over.

The worm beast had disappeared, and a new hole had appeared just below them.

"All gone," said Apollo.

'That's amazing," said Tetra. "Where did you say you were from?"

"Oh, it's wossname... the deep," replied Apollo. "I'm an anglerfish, there's lots of us there. We all have lights to help see us through the day."

"Thanks," murmured Tantalus, sucking on his sore flipper.

"What's the deep?" asked Tetra.

"Where the water is at its deepest and darkest, I guess," replied Apollo. "It's a little tight living but if you visit, don't leave without trying the wossname... the local food!"

"Food?" murmured Tantalus, still sucking on his flipper.

Tetra gave Tantalus an eyebrow raise and then sighed.

"I guess we should make our way to the coral reef" said Tetra while tugging Tantalus on his flipper.

"As you wish," replied the anglerfish. "Lots of white walls though. Nothing living there. Strange really, I always thought there would be more creatures up here than back home. I seem to be so wrong."

"Captain said there would be…"

"Captain?" asked Apollo.

"Never mind," Tetra said and smiled. "We should be on our way. Thanks for all your help!"

"My pleasure," said Apollo, before scooting away, singing his song.

Tetra and Tantalus carried on over the sand, where the holes were now more frequent than the fish themselves. It had been a long journey, but the white line on the horizon was now much thicker, and it soon became apparent what Apollo had meant.

The white walls were now in perfect view.

Chapter 16
White Walls

A small shoal of fish swam towards them. They didn't stop, nor did they seem to notice Tetra or Tantalus. They fluttered by like the wind had picked up a group of leaves and was dragging them somewhere else.

They were peculiar though. Their eyes were white and their scales were a faded orange; almost like the rain had washed the paint away. In between the faded orange, dabs of grey flickered between like a poorly sketched drawing that had been half rubbed out.

"Is this the way to the coral reef?" Tetra tried to ask them, to which only silence was the answer.

"It's no use," said Tantalus. "These fiwsh seem a ghost of their former selves."

A branch of coral floated past them, following the shoal of fish. It was pink, or at least it used to be, for only a hint of pink remained. Mostly it was now white, brittle to the touch and hollow on the inside.

They swam a little further in the opposite direction to the fish to a small mound, where the sunlight sparkled beneath the surface. A white wall could be seen. As they moved closer, the white wall became less impressive and appeared more desolate. It wasn't really a wall, nor anything that had once been a building, but crumbled and brittle pieces of white coral that had gathered on the edge of the coral reef.

As Tetra and Tantalus entered the reef, it wasn't just the wall that was white, but everything inside was too. The only hints of colour that did exist seemed to be fading before their eyes and, within moments, bright pinks and flamboyant oranges had become as pale as the fish themselves.

"I thought coral reefs were colourful," said Tetra.

"They used to be when I was younger," said Tantalus.

"What happened to this one?" Tetra asked Tantalus.

"No idea," Tantalus shrugged. "Although, it does feel warmer here than it did before."

"It's a ghost town," said Tetra. "Look at that eel hiding over there, he looks like a ghost."

"Eels were always cweepy to me anyway," chuckled Tantalus. "I can't see the diffewence!"

"Something is wrong, that's for sure," said Tetra.

They waded through the bones of the coral, and not even a sting could be felt on their skin. It broke and snapped as they pushed through the thickest parts, and curled away from them in the thinner parts. If not for the white coral, the place would have been as deserted as the desert where they had met the shark. Oddly, the desert felt preferable to Tetra, at least something was alive there. Even the life here felt dead.

Where the coral almost scraped the surface, a blue bulge lay between some of the branches. As Tetra and Tantalus approached, they could see that it was more than just a bulge. It was sturdy fabric sewn together in curvaceous shape, with the emblem of the ship's flag planted in its centre.

"The captain's hat!" yelled Tetra. "And I haven't had to fight either a hydra or a finless shark to get it."

She swam closer cautiously, but indeed, there was not a hydra or a finless shark, no tentacles, no teeth, not even a worm trying to stop her. But such had been Tetra's adventure so far, that she felt a sense of uncertainty. Even when the hat was within arm's reach, she couldn't be sure there wasn't some kind of trap.

She checked each branch of coral and every grain of sand around the hat, but nothing felt amiss. The sand was still sand and the coral was still dead. And the hat – most of all the hat – remained between the branches of coral.

"Is something wrong?" Tantalus asked loudly in the distance.

"I don't know," Tetra said. "Don't you think this is a bit too easy?"

"Easy is good," said Tantalus. "Easy is perhaps the most dewicious of them all."

"I want to agree," said Tetra. "But something's still making me unsure."

She moved her hand towards the hat. The hat, as still as ever, lay in wait as her hand lightly touched its fabric. Her fingers began to clench, bending to grip the hat, and as her fingers tightened, the hat began to move. When the hat moved, Tetra pulled away, but she couldn't pull away quick enough. From beneath the hat itself, a small claw arose and pinched her hand.

"Ouch!" she screamed. "I knew it! I knew it!" she yelled, watching the hat scuttle away into underneath a large piece of coral.

"Your hat is getting away," said Tantalus, pointing towards the scuttling hat.

"I know," whined Tetra, as she began to chase after it.

The hat was now buried deep within the coral. But the coral was still brittle, and without much thought, Tetra began ripping through it like the hydra through the forest.

"I need that hat!" she yelled. "This sea has used up all my patience."

"Go away," a voice said from beneath the hat. "This is my home, find your own."

Tetra didn't listen, or perhaps she didn't hear, as she tore through the coral until she was within arm's length with the hat once more. Without any hesitation this time, she grabbed the hat and turned it over, and there inside the hat sat a small crab, snapping its pincers.

"I said leave me alone!" shouted the crab. "Finders keepers."

"This is not your hat," said Tetra. "This is the captain's hat."

"I've lived in this hat for nearly six months," said the crab, trying to pull the hat away from Tetra. "I will not give it up, not for any price."

"I'm sure you can find another home," said Tetra, pulling at the hat. "Maybe a shell or even a nice rock."

"Look around you, kid," said the crab. "Everything that once had a shell is long dead."

"I'm not dead," said Tantalus, raising his flipper.

"No one's talking about you," said the crab. "You really want this hat, huh?"

"I need this hat," said Tetra, pulling with all her might. "It's my only way back home."

"Maybe we can strike some kind of deal," said the crab. He let go of the hat and Tetra fell back into some coral. The hat slowly fell back down to the ground and back onto the crab's back.

"What kind of deal?" asked Tetra.

"You may have noticed this coral reef isn't the place it once was," said the crab. "It used to be vibrant, full of life, full of adventure. There were so many shells that no crab needed to fight over a house. We all lived in luxury."

"What happened?" asked Tetra, closely following behind the crab.

"The sea suddenly started getting warmer," said the crab, snapping off some coral into his pincers. "You see this coral? It used to be home to many different creatures, but now it couldn't even stop a jellyfish invasion."

"Jellyfwish?" asked Tantalus.

"Yeah, yeah, yeah, turtles eat jellyfish," said the crab. "But anyway, I need you two to go to the ice walls north of here, and bring back a giant ice cube. It might help cool the sea and bring my friends home again."

"Where did they go?" asked Tetra.

"In search of some kind of lagoon," said the crab. "I told them it was a myth, but they didn't believe me. Something about there being more profit away from here now. Greedy crabs, never content with their shells."

"I knew getting this hat wouldn't be easy," sighed Tetra, rolling on her back and placing her hands behind her head. "I am so fed up."

"Well, if you can't help me…" said the crab. "I supposed I'll be keeping my hat."

"Fine," Tetra sighed once more. "We will travel to this ice wall of yours."

"Pinch on it?" said the crab, stretch out his claw.

Tetra nervously stretch at her hand towards the crab's claw. When she was an inch away from the claw, the crab merely tapped her hand with his claw and winked at her.

"I wouldn't pinch you again," said the crab. "You soft bodies can't handle it. My name is Hermes. Now that we're in agreement, it is right to be acquainted."

"I'm Tetra," she replied.

"And I am Tantalus," said the turtle, holding up his flipper.

"That's great, that's great," said Hermes. "With such a lucrative deal for both of us, it's only fair I offer you exceptional hospitality. Stay the night in the coral reef and be on your way in the morning."

The white rocks provided a shelter from the steady current that drifted around the edges. Tetra and Tantalus settled into the broken bones of the coral reef. It was uncomfortable, but after an exhausting day, Tetra managed to catch a few hours' sleep.

Before the sunlight could sprinkle across the white walls of the reef, Tetra and Tantalus were already on their way to the far north – where the sea is so cold it freezes. As they travelled close to the surface, the sand below them was becoming further and further away.

Chapter 17
Glittering Trails

There was water to the east, water to the west and water in every other direction imaginable. Be-neath them, the seabed had long since disappeared, only the dark depths of more water remained. The sea was cooler, like a fresh spring running down the side of a mountain, which to Tetra's annoyance, Tantalus wouldn't stop complaining about.

"It sure is chilwy up here," shivered Tantalus.

"It's only going to get colder, so you better get used to it," said Tetra.

"Yeah," sighed Tantalus, and briefly paused. "It sure is getting colder up here."

"Will you stop it?" asked Tetra. "The quicker we get this ice cube, the quicker we can get back to the warmer waters, and then I can hopefully go home."

"I'm surpwised any creature can call live in these chilwy waters," said Tantalus, glancing around as a cloud of krill danced in the distance, swooshing in the open space like a plastic bag lost in the wind.

"Have you ever seen so many krill before?" Tetra asked Tantalus.

"I've seen many difwerent cwustaceans," chuckled Tantalus, his beak widening as his eyes followed the cloud of krill. "Some of that are quite dewicious if you catch them while they're soft. Others have left me with a nasty pinch and one even smacked me with its fwist. But never have I seen so many at once."

"I wonder where they're going," Tetra whispered, as she gently swam towards them.

"Oh, you'll never catch kwill like that," chuckled Tantalus, as he swooped in behind her, flinging her onto his shell. Tantalus leapt forward, accelerating towards the krill, and as he spun into the swarm, they repelled away like a shadow avoids the light.

And when Tetra and Tantalus were amongst the krill, such was the thickness of the swarm, that it could have been night and they wouldn't have known. Like a volcano erupting and leaving ash in the sky, or even a blizzard fumbling across a frozen wilderness, the swarm of krill blanketed the open sea like a dense fog would cloud an open field.

"This reminds me of my childhood," chuckled Tantalus.

"How so?" asked Tetra.

"I remember the skwies being this dense when I hatched," chuckled Tantalus. "It's any wonder I even made it to the sea at all."

"What happened?" asked Tetra.

"Seagulls and pelicans: sky wats," chuckled Tantalus. "My shell wasn't always this hard, you know. Back then, I would have made an easy dinner."

Tantalus slowed a little and gulped towards the sky. "Many of my bwothers and sisters never made it."

"That's terrible," said Tetra, with a slight tear running down her cheek.

"I only made it by chance," Tantalus chuckled with watery eyes. "A big wave hit me before the sky wat could take me. Sadly my sister behind me was taken instead."

"I'm so sorry," said Tetra with her head resting against Tantalus' shell.

"Not your fault," chuckled Tantalus. "These aren't sky wats anyway, harmwess kwill."

They flew beneath the krill and, as they dived, strange mountains staggered far beneath the depths. They cut through the sea like a serrated blade would a tough steak, then at its end, the sharpest of all the peaks stood reaching agonisingly towards the surface. As the krill bent around the peaks, a strange glow emitted from the side of the mountain.

The mountain was tall, at least it must have been as its bottom could not be seen. In the dark depths below, grumbles could be heard, like a deep whine weaving through the valleys of the underworld. Tetra gulped, stared down and shuddered at the thought of what must exist that far below. She looked back up towards the glow, and there near the peak of the mountain was a small crack on its side.

Tantalus swam towards the crack at speeds that would make a barracuda blush. Inside, what made the crack glow was quite unexpected. Pockets of strange algae, no larger than the size of nautilus shell, shone brighter than the moon on a crisp, cloudless night. Around each corner was a new glow, emitting a different light, sparkling the cave inside like the aurora lights.

"This place reminds me of the forest," said Tetra, her eyes widening as she swam around the glowing algae. "You know, the mushrooms."

"I'm getting a more gwoomy feeling," jittered Tantalus.

"What do you mean?" asked Tetra. "The forest was gloomy."

"It's a wittle colder in here than there, and I don't think it's just the northern sea," said Tanta-lus.

"Look!" exclaimed Tetra, as she dashed deeper into the cave. "This place could go on for miles."

She wandered through, paddling like a bewildered puppy on its first walk in a forest. She gazed at each alga, glowing more vividly the further inside the cave. Some even draped down the sides, like drawn curtains hiding either the outside or the inside.

"I'm not sure we should be going this deep," said Tantalus, his voice echoing through the cave.

"Relax, this is probably the safest place we've been so far," said Tetra, glancing around as the light shimmered across every rock and sparkled above every grain of sand.

"Why do I get the fweeling I'm going to disagree?" gulped Tantalus.

"Well, there's no way a hydra could fit in this cave," said Tetra. "And there's no way that shark could fit in here either!"

"What about a skeweton?" gulped Tantalus.

"I've never even seen Captain Neureus' skeleton leave his ship," said Tetra, raising her hands in the air in frustration.

"This place sure looks like a place Captain Neureus would hide in," said Tantalus, slowly touching one of the glowing algae with his flipper. "It's probably where he hides his treasure."

"You really like to stereotype pirates," said Tetra, turning around to face Tantalus and raising her eyebrow.

"You saw his cwew on the deck," said Tantalus, shrugging his flippers out wide. "They weren't exactly offering a cwuise around some exotic islands."

"They might be a little rough around the edges…" said Tetra, her eyes once more focused on the array of different lights reflecting across the cave walls. "But I'm not expecting a comfortable ride home, I just need to get there."

They swam deeper into the cave until they arrived at a junction. One route went left, which was brightly lit by the glowing algae. The other route, which leant to the right, was much darker. The water slowly flowed from the dark path and down into the brightly lit path, a stream that was slightly cooler than the rest of the sea around it.

"Well, I know my choice," said Tantalus.

"I guess it seems an easy decision to make," said Tetra.

"You agree we should turn back and forget about the ice cube?" said Tantalus.

"Of course not," said Tetra, drifting slowly towards the left tunnel. "There are even more beautiful colours this way."

Tetra wandered down the tunnel while Tantalus followed closely behind. The light of the algae seemed to swirl like the northern lights would around a cold, wintry sky. There was a rhythm to their madness, like an orchestra made of light rather than sound, playing a melody not for the ears but the eyes.

There were few twists and turns, but it was mostly straight and narrow without an end. But Tetra didn't want an end, at least not right away. Everything was mesmerising, even more mesmerising than before. Even when small rocks tumbled down the cave walls, she didn't flinch nor tremble, she moved towards the light and down into an endless pit of wonder.

Time stood still, or it felt like it did. The sun could not be seen above the cave walls, nor could it peek through the cracks or the holes. For Tetra, life outside the cave could almost be forgotten. But it was not forgotten, for even in these moments of beauty, cold water would slip past her neck and bring her back to reality.

The corridor tumbled through, becoming narrower and slightly darker. The algae still glowed, and when Tetra stared at it directly, it did so with the same intensity. But, somehow, the cave felt now more sombre than before.

Stones fell from the walls. There were gullies where other stones had fallen before and rolled across the floor, each gully deeper and wider than one the one before it. The water felt warmer on Tetra's skin, sometimes warmer than the bath back home.

"TURN AROUND!"

"Who said that?" Tetra called out towards the darkness.

"I think we should do as it says," trembled Tantalus, already turning and quietly paddling away.

"We haven't got this far to turn around now," said Tetra. "There must be something at the end of this cave."

"I tend to find big jaws in dark pwaces," trembled Tantalus.

"*LEAVE NOW!*"

Big, green eyes bobbled out from the darkness of the cave. They skittled around, until they found Tetra and Tantalus. They then focused intensely on the duo without a single blink, much like a telescope zooming in on the nearest island.

Underneath the eyes, a large, red claw, shaped like a mullet, rose out from the rocks. Tantalus dived towards Tetra and pushed her behind a rock.

Just in time too. From the claw, a huge current propelled all the way down the tunnel. And when they came out from behind the rock, they noticed the water was now much warmer.

"*YOU MUST LEAVE NOW!*"

"Why?" shouted out Tetra, swimming towards the claw.

"What are you doing?" whispered Tantalus. "That's a massive fwist!"

Out from the darkness, the two eyes bobbled into the light once more. Soon, long whiskers, as vibrant as a rainbow, flowed out of the darkness, and then too the rest of its face. It was about the size of the shark, only bulkier, with huge claws and many legs.

"*YOU MUST LEAVE! YOUR CLUMSY FLIPPERS WILL RUIN MY HOME!*"

Then without a moment's notice, it raised its claw once more and aimed another jet of water towards them. This time they were caught and it pushed them across the tunnel. They whizzed past the junction and down the other route.

The other route was shorter, at least it felt so because of the speed of the jet. They came through to the end and out of the mountain.

Here, the water was cooler. Much colder in fact. Indeed, bits of ice floated across the surface. Tetra and Tantalus turned to look at each other, silent in their shock, and disorientated in their new surroundings. There were somehow outside the cave and somewhere completely different.

Chapter 18
Ice Walls

There was a wall. It stretched from the tip of the surface, all the way to the dark depths of the sea. To the west, it faded into the shadows, and to the east it dwindled into the shade. It glistened beneath the sunrise, and when a wave rolled above it, it twinkled like a thousand stars.

"It's kind of beautiful," said Tetra, placing her hand onto its surface. "But extremely cold. This wall is made from ice."

"Ice you say..." Tantalus said, swimming forward. "What is this ice stuff?"

"Frozen water," said Tetra, raising her eyebrow at the turtle. "You never seen ice before?"

"I've never been so far north," chuckled Tantalus. "Much too cold."

"I wonder who built this wall," said Tetra, inspecting the wall. "It seems to be melting in places."

"That's the opposite of me," jittered Tantalus, shivering with his flippers wrapped around his belly. "Even inside my shell is fweezing."

"I wonder what's behind this wall?" said Tetra.

"Beats me," said Tantalus. "I guess we will have to turn back and—"

"I'm sure there will be a gate or something somewhere," interrupted Tetra, swimming alongside the giant wall.

Further along, small jellyfish bobbled near the top of the wall. They were more translucent and Tetra nearly swam into them, only for Tantalus to call her name before she could. They were no bigger than her hands, and there were many, at least two dozen of them, hanging around what appeared to be a small crack in the wall.

"Do you see that?" asked Tetra.

"Oh, I see it alwight," said Tantalus, licking his lips and moving closer towards the crack.

"The crack…" said Tetra, her eyes following Tantalus as he moved closer. "Oh no, not the—"

Before Tetra could finish her words, Tantalus had begun gobbling up all the jellyfish he could see. One after another, he stuck out his giant tongue and swooped all the small jellyfish into his enormous mouth, apart from one, hidden deep in the crack. Tantalus' eyes bulged larger, and with every moving second, he edged closer towards the crack.

"Just one more…" Tantalus whispered.

"I don't think that's a good idea," said Tetra.

"Welax," said Tantalus, licking his lips one more time. "I've gotten jellyfwish out of all kinds of knocks and cwannies. If anything, this one will be the easiest one of all!"

Tantalus flung his tongue towards the crack, much like a hungry chameleon would towards a grasshopper. It spiralled at a great pace towards a crack that appeared increasingly small as his tongue drew closer. And when his tongue hit, Tantalus' eyes grew wider.

The jellyfish slowly bobbled away, deeper into the crack and perhaps onto the other side of the wall. Tantalus hadn't reached the jellyfish, not even close, indeed, his tongue hadn't even entered the small crack. He was instead licking the ice wall, but, rather than eating the ice wall, Tantalus' tongue was very much stuck to it.

"Hewp…" mumbled Tantalus.

"I told you that was a bad idea," said Tetra.

"I didn't know ice was sticky," he mumbled, as he pulled as hard as he could on the ice.

"You think too much about your belly," huffed Tetra, as she grabbed his shell and tried to pull him. "Always hungry."

But no matter how hard they tried, Tantalus' tongue wouldn't budge. They tried pulling him away from the wall, but it hurt his tongue too much. Tetra tried chiselling at the wall with a stone, but the wall was much too hard. Tetra even tried making Tantalus drool by talking about jellyfish, but his saliva only froze when it touched the ice wall.

"This is hopeless!" yelled Tetra. "Why did you have to try eat the jellyfish?"

"I get hungwy," mumbled Tantalus.

Tetra floated in thought. This was the oddest conundrum she had yet to come across. She might have escaped from a rampaging hydra and hid from an angry shark, but Tantalus getting himself stuck was perhaps the most confusing problem of all.

As it happened, she didn't need to think for long. Before she could ponder another minute, the walls began to shake. As they shook, the walls crumbled, and where the crack had been small, it became much larger. With a leap backwards, Tantalus found himself free from the ice wall as the crack became more of a large hole. As the shaking stopped, Tetra and Tantalus floated in front of the once grand wall and peered into the giant hole.

"Well, at least I can finish my dinner," said Tantalus

"No," said Tetra. "I'd rather you left that jellyfish."

"You're probably wight," said Tantalus. "I'm assuming you want us to go through the hole?"

"I am curious what's behind it," said Tetra. "Although a piece of the ice wall would be a large enough ice cube for Hermes."

"You first," said Tantalus, pushing her towards the hole with his giant flipper.

Through the large hole and past the white walls revealed something spectacular, something Tetra had never thought she would ever see below the sea. A mountain of ice carved delicately, with tiny holes that looked like doors, and winding pebbles between that looked like roads. And high above, on top of it all, a building much like a castle, with shadowing towers and glistening walls of white. An ice city of sorts built for those that were small.

"This city is beautiful," gleamed Tetra, with her mouth wide open. "But it is rather small. I wonder what could possibly live here?"

"I'm surprised anything could," shivered Tantalus. "It's even colder here than outside the wall."

They glided above the city, checking out its winding paths and its intricate buildings. Up close, each house appeared like a miniature igloo, with tiny ice bricks put together to craft a wondrous abode. They were layered, houses on top of houses, delicately built like a fancy cake with the delicious frosting.

But unlike the town back home, or any city Tetra had seen before in books, this city was empty. In fact, empty didn't explain it at all. Not even vacant would be the word to describe this city. It was like a vacuum in space, or better yet, a vacuum beneath the waves.

"*Shhh!* Do you hear that?" asked Tetra

"You mean waves wolling above?" chuckled Tantalus.

"No," said Tetra, as she slowly drifted towards the castle. "I hear something... maybe even someone."

"This place is about as empty as my belly was last night," chuckled Tantalus. "Not even algae can gwow on its walls."

Tetra began peering through all the windows in the castle, but each room was empty, without a crab or a fish in sight. Just empty beds and empty chairs, empty tables and empty stairs. Even the large hall at the front of the even larger hall appeared empty. But the sound was much clearer, and indeed, it did sound like a voice.

"I think someone is crying," said Tetra.

"I'm sorry," said Tantalus. "I get awfully emotional when thinking about food."

"Not you," said Tetra. "Someone inside the castle."

"I can't see anyone inside the castle," said Tantalus, moving in closer to get a better look. "Maybe there are bigger windows around this side."

As Tantalus turned, his flippers kicked back against the castle. Its once proud and mighty roof began to waver, cracking down the middle and slowly sliding away from both Tetra and Tantalus.

"Oh no..." said Tetra, her mouth wide open, watching the roof avalanche towards the rest of the city.

"Oops!" said Tantalus, nervously smiling as the roof disappeared before their eyes. "But at least we can see easier inside now," he chuckled.

The crying was louder than it had been before; not so muffled. It was still rather quiet to Tetra's human ears though. She went right up to the now-broken wall and peeked her nose over to see what was inside.

There was a huge room in the middle, chiselled from diamond-like ice, with pearls and gems adorning each wall. A long rug, which looked like it was made from the algae that shone in the cave, lay across the floor, leading via a small row of stairs onto a higher platform. Two thrones stood on this platform, one was empty, while the other was occupied by a small, sobbing shrimp.

Chapter 19
A Royal Welcome

Surrounded by broken ice and tattered silk, the shrimp sat staring at the floor, never looking up towards Tetra and Tantalus. He sighed into his throne's arm rest; his pearly crown slanted across his head. His whiskers were tattered like an old rug, and his claws were mangled like a gnawed lobster.

"Everything is lost," the shrimp muttered, his words as quiet as a bubble drifting over the horizon. He slumped further down in his throne, his claw pressed against his cheek, and his eyes half covered by his crown. "There is nothing left here."

"What happened?" Tetra blurted out from above, her whole face now peering over the palace.

The shrimp jumped out of his throne and darted around frantically before resting hidden behind a tattered silk curtain.

"Guards! Guards!" He bellowed into the empty room. "There must be at least one guard left," he pleaded into the curtain.

"And I thought I lacked subtlwety," said Tantalus, patting Tetra on her back with his large flipper.

"You don't know unless you ask," said Tetra to Tantalus. She then leaned her head inside the palace. "We're not here to harm you, we were just curious," she echoed into the vast chamber.

"Actually, only you were cuwious," muttered Tantalus. "I'm fweezing my fwippers off up here."

The curtains shook frantically as the shrimp peered his head around the side and looked around cautiously.

"Whatever you want, take it," said the shrimp, sketching his gaze around the room.

"Oh, there's nothing we need from you," said Tetra, beaming her warmest smile towards the little shrimp below her.

"*Gah!*" he squealed. "I'm only small, one of me would never fill your belly."

"You got that wight," said Tantalus, folding his flippers. "I never had a taste for shwimp, the shell is too cwunchy and wequires too much of effort to—"

"Seriously?" interrupted Tetra. "And you said I lack subtlety?"

"You were the one that scawed him first," Tantalus argued back.

"Well, now he's scared he's going to be eaten by you," Tetra fought back.

"Of course, he's not! I just told him I don't like shwimp!" said Tantalus.

"Oh, what use is hiding!" cried the shrimp, floating slowly out from behind the curtains. "Everything is gone, I might as well be gone too." He slumped back onto his throne, stretched out his claws, and held his head below his neck.

"What's he doing?" whispered Tantalus, gently nudging Tetra with his flipper.

"I think he's the last one," said Tetra, her eyes filling with a sorrow of dew. Then she called out to the shrimp, "We didn't come this far north to hurt you. We came looking for a giant ice cube."

"Oh, just take a piece of the great wall," said the shrimp, still slumped with his back towards Tetra and Tantalus. "I wish to be left alone."

Tantalus began rubbing his flippers, beaming a smile from one side of his cheek to the other. He turned to face the giant ice wall in the distance, gave Tetra a nudge and began paddling towards the wall while whistling a happy tune.

"Wait, Tantalus," said Tetra, staring into the broken palace as she had once done with the fish bowl. "I think we should help him."

Tantalus' whistling slowed to a sudden long whine, as he turned to face Tetra. His face was green, at least more green than usual, and even the algae on his shell seemed to droop alongside his flippers. He reluctantly paddled back towards Tetra, his flippers flailing at his side, and murmuring something incomprehensible.

Above, ice drifted like a glacier carving a path down a mountainside. It flowed over the city and towards the other side of the great wall, where another large gap appeared. Indeed, on closer inspection, the great wall was a great oval, encircling the city to either keep something in, or to keep something out. Either way, it was severely compromised, and it seemed to Tetra, what was bothering the shrimp must be closely linked to the wall's destruction.

"What's your name?" asked Tetra.

The shrimp arose from his knees, his eyes glistening in the shadows of the frozen drift. His mouth widened and his whiskers curled as they tightened. The tears from his eyes froze into hail droplets, and when the current flowed across the palace, it wiped them from his cheeks and carried them towards the ice above. He looked at both Tetra and Tantalus and quietly smiled. "I am sorry, as you can see, I haven't been at my best recently. My name is Anteros, King Anteros."

"Do we bow or what?" whispered Tantalus while nudging Tetra, causing her to frown momentarily before regaining her composure.

"So, what happened here?" asked Tetra.

"You really don't know, do you?" said King Anteros. "The walls used to protect us from the outside. The outside is dangerous.

It's filled with gigantic beasts that I'm sure you've already seen a few of them."

"More than a few," gulped Tetra.

"Then you understand," said King Anteros. "It was like living in our own glass bottle. We could see the outside, the outside could see us, but it couldn't harm us. But then the waters became warmer and the wall began to melt."

"You mean it used to be colder than this?" asked Tantalus, shivering from his shell unto his flipper.

"Oh, it used to be beautifully crisp," said the king, holding his claws up high as if he could touch the sky. "I remember as a young fry, every winter there was solid ice above us, without a single bit of light for months."

"Doesn't sound partwicularly dewicious," mumbled Tantalus.

The king turned away, stared down at his throne, and then looked back up to the sky. Tears like crystals fell once more. Droplets that didn't disappear into the surrounding water but had a life of their own, slowly settling on the ground below. He turned to face Tetra and Tantalus once more and gave a smile that seemed showered by sadness.

"It's been a month that has felt like one long day," King Anteros said. "When the walls weakened, our fears grew stronger. The unknown started to become our reality, and when it knocked, we crumbled."

He picked up a piece of decorative silk from the floor, it was torn and ragged, with shreds hanging on by a mere thread. But it was also beautiful, a blue as deep as the ocean with pinks and greens as diverse as the Milky Way. It was, however, a piece of a once enormous banner, that would have stretched across the whole room. And when the king's eyes turned towards the wall, Tetra saw its tattered remains still hanging.

"Cities can be rebuilt," said the king, as another tear wept into the sea. "Even banners as glorious as this one, however torn, can be remade. But a heart, once broken, can never beat in the same way again."

There was a pause: a moment so brief that a wave didn't have time to crash, nor did a tear have the time to fall. Tetra's eyes gazed into King Anteros' eyes, and as his little legs sunk slightly into the sand, small particles slowly rose into what would become a cloud. And when the moment unpaused, the king lifted his head and sighed into the depths of his own despair.

"It should have been me," said the king. "When the Boreas came, it should have been me."

"Boreas?" asked Tetra.

"You really don't know where you are, do you?" asked the king, to which Tetra leaned back with her eyebrows slightly raised. "This sea is plagued by the Boreas. The walls were built to keep her out, but when they melted, she found her way in."

"She destroyed the city?" asked Tetra.

"She consumed the city," said the king. "Every shrimp, fry or elder, swallowed with one giant gulp." He turned his back and looked back up at the tattered banner. "No doubt other kingdoms have suffered the same fate. I am most likely the last of my kind."

"Didn't we see a swarm on our way up here?" pondered Tantalus, with his flipper on his chin.

"Weren't they krill?" asked Tetra.

"Krill, Shrimp, Krill," said the king. "Differences are minimal in the face of annihilation. The krill you saw are probably long lost at this point. So, please take any ice you need; I won't be needing it where I'm going."

"Where is it you're going?" asked Tetra.

"There's no life for me here," said the king, not answering the question. "I will follow the ice over the horizon, and there may I find Boreas and join my shrimps."

"Well, that sounds like a bad idea," said Tantalus, frowning. "It's much better to eat the dinner than be the dinner."

"Easy for you to say, my hard-shelled friend," said the king. "Anyway, please take all the ice you need and leave me in peace."

Tetra felt taken aback, she didn't like to be told what to do. She especially didn't like it when her mum told her what to do. But this shrimp was a king, and for all his sadness, it was his decision to make. She signalled to Tantalus to leave and they did so with much haste.

There were plenty of blocks of ice to choose from but, for all their determination, one that would be big enough for Hermes turned out be too heavy for both of them. They certainly couldn't come back and forth with small chunks; the journey up was much too long and the voyage back already seemed a daunting task.

It was then though, as they toiled, that the ice broke again. A loud song, with a chorus as beautiful as it was treacherous, vibrated across the walls and resonated them until they cracked. Then, in the distance, a giant shadow came tumbling over the horizon.

Chapter 20
A Lonely Orchestra

The sound of a lonely orchestra reverberated around the fallen city; an empty palace indulging in its own self-pity. The melody of the waves above accompanied the choir resonating from the shadow in the distance. And when a huge mouth appeared, it didn't seem to belong to the monster that had been portrayed, but to a friendly face in immense pain.

So big was this creature that, as it approached the city, it shrouded all below in complete darkness. It echoed its song of sorrow with a deafening melody that would have hurt if it hadn't felt so beautiful. As much as Tetra wanted to cover her ears with her hands, she couldn't. She wanted to hear it, even though the sound moved her in terrible ways.

Its large dorsal fin scraped the surface of the water, creating a screech as it scratched along the barrier. Then it dove towards the city, flipping its caudal fin against the barrier which created a large rumble across the city. During its descent, Tetra saw a golden spear dug into its back. A trail of red flurried from where it had buried into the creature's skin.

Before Tetra could cast a whisper, she was dragged away by Tantalus to the edge of the city. Tetra turned to face the palace and as she did, an earthquake rumbled, tearing the walls down around them.

A gigantic tail, more conspicuous than the full moon on dark night, stood above the dust cloud that washed around the city. A trail of misery lay before Tetra's widening eyes. And as the tail swung towards the seabed, it swirled debris around like a ladle in a soup. What was cooking wasn't edible, nor was it particularly warm in this frozen now-wasteland. It was just a fallen kingdom being swept beneath the sea.

"I never liked whales," remarked Tantalus. "I've seen a choir of them sing a mountain to the gwound."

"Do you think he's OK?" asked Tetra.

"The whale will be just dandy," said Tantalus. "Like fwesh jelly served on a bed of fwowers."

"No," said Tetra. "King Anteros."

"Oh," said Tantalus. "I'm not really sure he was OK to begin with."

As the carnage settled, with dust and ice sinking towards the seabed, Tetra slowly drifted closer to the centre of the city. It had been a glorified ruin before, perhaps like the city of Atlantis, if it had ever existed. And it certainly had the forgotten city under the sea vibe going now. But, instead of crumbling stone withstanding the tide, there was mostly sand and the occasional rubble.

When Tantalus caught up with Tetra, he tried to convince her to turn back. The walls were safe, at least safer than the open wound of the city. But Tetra could not hear, or at least she didn't want to hear. The song of the whale now had no echo, and it was all that Tetra could feel through every bone of her body. And when she looked up, the whale's tail was already a shadow in the distance.

Beneath the sand, a small clam clapped a steady beat. To its beat, a shrub of sorts, as green as it was blue, swayed in rhythm. The voice of the lonely orchestra still sung across the ocean, and the sea still danced along with its whisper.

Tetra stumbled across the rubble. Much of the palace was now flat, and Tantalus was keen to remind Tetra that their part in destroying the roof was now irrelevant. Indeed, Tantalus was right.

Where the roof had once fallen in, the rest of the palace now lay on top. All that stood were two empty thrones, part of the tapestry caught on the heel of each leg.

There was no current, the sea was as still as a puddle on a quiet roadside. The tapestry sunk sullen towards the ground. There was no movement, not even a sound beyond the gentle song in the distance. And yet, Tetra felt like there were a hundred eyes all focused on her as she approached the tapestry.

She picked up the sunken cloth and flicked off any sand that slept on it. Amongst the intricate patterns of shells and seaweed was something she recognised. Curiously, on the tapestry, that something seemed much more alive; there was a sail without a rip, and a plank without a hole. Tetra was sure that what she could see was the captain's ship.

Further along, spears, or maybe even harpoons, flew from the ship. One of which became embedded in a large whale, to which even the tapestry could be heard singing a song of sadness. The tapestry ended where the tip of a large tentacle emerged, covered in red and a faint smell of burning of wood.

"I see history is repeating itself," coughed a recognisable voice form beneath the rubble. Tantalus pushed away a few stones and from beneath stumbled an out-of-breath King Anteros. "It's been a long time since I've stared at this tapestry," he choked.

"What does it mean?" asked Tetra.

"It's a tale passed down from shrimp to shrimp," said the king. "The tapestry was ripped long before the whale came to eat us. But I like to believe this is how it ends."

"I know that ship," said Tetra, still staring at the tapestry.

"Really?" said the king. "That would be surprising. This tapestry is over two hundred years old. That's two hundred generations of shrimps that lived and died without witnessing the ship."

"I know that ship," Tetra repeated once more.

"Whatever you say," said the king, now slumping back in his throne. "This room sure has changed. Without the walls, it has a unique perspective on my kingdom."

"The harpoon," said Tetra. "That must belong to the captain!"

"Oh no," said Tantalus, waving his flippers. "No, no, no! No more adventures. Let's get back to that gweedy cwab with the ice cube and be on our way."

But it was, as every day had been so far, not Tantalus' day. For when Tetra and Tantalus had a disagreement, it was never like the tide, or even a wave. It was much more like a river with everything flowing in one direction. And that river happened to be flowing in the direction of the whale and not the crab.

They began to travel further north, with an eager Tetra leading the way followed by a hesitant turtle. They weren't alone though, for the king himself felt a need to go too.

Tantalus shivered and his beak jittered. Icicles were forming on his flippers and he was sure to remind Tetra of this unfortunate situation every ten seconds or so. In fact, even Tetra felt cold. She wouldn't tell Tantalus, but even she was starting to regret pursuing the whale.

There were chunks of ice, as big as the whale itself, floating gently around the sea. In one chunk, a shark was frozen solid, its teeth grinning as they paddled past. Another chunk had seemingly captured a poor octopus, while another seemed to trap an elephant, although this one wore a reddened fur.

Tantalus gulped at every creature he saw in the ice. Each time a new one floated by, he pointed towards it with his flipper, reminding Tetra that that would be them if they didn't leave immediately. It was difficult for Tetra to hear him though because the more ice that bobbled past them, the more the whale's song reverberated around them.

As the sea became colder, the song became louder. Two sunken icebergs were bouncing off the barrier, unable to float as the sea had intended them to. In between them, the song ricocheted off their walls and danced around Tetra's ears.

The lonely orchestra was now in full chorus. In front of Tetra's eyes, the enormous creature hovered gracefully, singing into the northern wintry seas. Tetra, mesmerised, slowly paddled closer to the whale, and as she did, a small creature whizzed past her head.

"I'm coming for you, Eros!" he said. Tetra looked behind her to find a half-frozen Tantalus shivering out of his shell and a king that was no longer there.

"King Anteros!" she called but to no reply.

"He has gone after the whale on his own," shivered Tantalus. "Not sure when he became so bwave."

"We need to go get him," said Tetra as she swam faster towards the whale. Tantalus sighed and paddled along after her.

When they reached the whale, King Anteros was nowhere in sight. There was only a whale singing her song. Tetra knew she needed to find him, but first she had to get that harpoon so she could return it to the captain.

Chapter 21
Riding the Whale

A deafening moan roared across the ocean. It was so loud that Tetra could feel it enter her skin and then bounce between every cell in her body. She was, though, right next to the source, as it towered above her like a blimp would have, had it sailed the sea and not the sky.

The whale was obviously in pain. Even its sweet song, which had drawn Tetra towards her, was a song woven of sullen chords and morose melodies. On Tetra's home island, music was usually cheerful. A carnival, in fact. For Tetra, sad music wasn't normal, and normal usually displeased her, so maybe that's why she was drawn to such a unique arrangement of sounds.

But, nonetheless, there was a missing king and an unhappy whale. A whale that had a harpoon deep inside its skin that left a hazy crimson flow seeping from the wound. While Tantalus jittered in the distance, unwilling to come too close to a beast of this magnitude, Tetra began to slowly approach the lonesome whale.

"Easy," she said. "I just want to help you." Swimming above the whale, which took a few minutes due to the whale's gigantic size, she cautiously approached the harpoon. The whale was much like the moon. From a distance she glowed, an ever-lightening presence in the ocean sky. Up close, she was littered with crater-like wounds, as deep as Tetra was tall, and as wide as Tantalus' belly.

The harpoon itself was no rusty item of cutlery found on your grandma's kitchen table. It shone a delicate blue. with a severed rope dangling from its end. Strangely, it had its own aura, like it wasn't attached to the whale, nor had been attached to a ship before. In Tetra's mind, the harpoon was talking to her, but she couldn't hear words, nor translate its voice.

The voice was reassuring though, like a bold piece of chocolate asking to be unwrapped. She felt a desire to grasp the harpoon, and she wanted to resist the urge for fear of hurting the whale. However, the harpoon was irresistible. By the time she had considered how the whale would feel or react, her hands were already grasped onto the harpoon.

Tetra arose on a golden beach. There was nothing to be said other than the golden sand on her feet felt like home, but it wasn't home. Nothing around her could be said to be home. But it did feel so, and sometimes that's all that matters.

The sea was just as gold as the sand, and the only way to tell the difference between them was how they moved. The same could be said of the sky, though the sky didn't move. It seemed to shine without the sun.

In her hands, she still grasped the harpoon, although now it didn't look blue but golden. Something felt natural about the harpoon, much like how the waves try to reach the moon, or how the tide seeks the horizon.

And as she stared towards the horizon, she recognised fate approaching. It was a distant fate. A fate she had already met in the past. As if time itself had closed like the top of a bottle. It was the tsunami that had dragged her into the sea before, but this time it was as golden as the rest of the world.

Instinctively, Tetra raised her harpoon and aimed it towards the tsunami and, as it came crashing down, it carved the enormous tsunami clean in two. And it was only then, when the two halves dissipated, that she awakened to find her hands still gripped the harpoon and the harpoon was still in the whale's back. It was then that the ride got wild.

Tantalus flurried behind the whale as she erratically plunged down into the deeper depths of the ocean. She was singing in agony as Tetra held onto the harpoon. The harpoon was shining gold, giving a light in the depth's darkness, which Tantalus could follow.

"We need to get the harpoon out of her back!" shouted Tetra in Tantalus' direction.

"I'm having a hard enough time keeping up," he puffed back.

The dark depths were like the night sky, speckled with stars of their own, only these stars had entire personalities that seemed to snap back. In one instance, Tantalus could have sworn that one of the specks had sharp teeth, but it was too late to go back for a second look, nor would he have wanted to.

The golden light from the harpoon was strong enough to scare most of the specks away and, as the whale swam back up, the specks had all but disappeared. The whale was slowing and even her song slowed to a steadier beat. Tantalus was also slowing but more due to a belly full of jelly rather than a harpoon shoved through his back.

Tetra heard the voice of the harpoon whisper through her veins. It said nothing she could understand, but she felt it could understand her, almost like the harpoon knew who she was and what she was thinking.

"Perhaps you should let go," huffed Tantalus, unable to keep his breath for much longer.

"I can't!" she yelled back. "It won't let go of me!"

The harpoon jilted then, sliding a few inches out of the whale's skin. The whale growled another chord into the sea as white, icicle tears blossomed from her eyes. She halted and bellowed more melodies around her, one of which struck a sunken iceberg and split it into two. The power of the whale's voice turned Tetra's eyes blind and left a nauseous ringing in her ears.

It had been several minutes, but it felt like several hours. The ringing had faded from Tetra's ears, and the blindness had crept away and in front of her was a golden light shining from the harpoon. The whale had stopped too, out of breath, and, behind her, a turtle had also stopped and was even more out of breath.

In the near distance, two halves of a once giant sunken iceberg had drifted away from each other. They moved slowly, but Tetra had been blind long enough for them both to have made great strides on their solo journeys.

It was, though, the harpoon that had its own journey to continue. It glowed once more, and the light that radiated from it heated the water several degrees around Tetra. A current began to flow out from the wound of the whale and towards the horizon. It flickered Tetra's thick, black hair as the glow sparkled across her.

Tetra's hands began to heat up, but not enough to burn or blister her skin. Just enough for her feel it and wince. Her veins flowed like molten lava and her eyes burned like fire. The harpoon finally became loose and began to dislodge from the whale, leaving a thicker trail of red flowing into the current.

Tantalus watched on, his breath almost gathered and his belly rumbling like he hadn't eaten in nearly thirty minutes; it had, of course, been much longer, but Tantalus and gluttony came together like the sand and the sea.

The whale yelped once more, and in doing so, the harpoon was freed from her skin and safely in Tetra's hands.

"It's out!" yelled Tantalus. "Now let's get us out of here before the whale notices."

Tetra, though, was preoccupied. The glow from the harpoon was now more intense than it had even been in her dream. There were gold flashes everywhere, even the sky past the barrier had a bronze tinge to it. But most strikingly, Tetra herself had become golden.

Tetra glowed as she floated in the middle of the freezing ocean. Tantalus stared in disbelief, unable to say a word. The whale had descended to the dark depths, leaving a trail of red in its path. It was finally silent: the lonely orchestra had finished her set. There was nothing but the sound of nothing, as if the vacuum of space had taken every drop of sound with it.

She turned around and faced Tantalus, producing the deepest of sighs. She felt different but wasn't sure if she really was different. Emotions clashed inside her so ferociously that they cancelled each other out, causing a moment of emptiness. An emptiness that felt unbreakable, at least until Tantalus opened his beak.

"So, I guess there's nothing to be done about that shwimp king, then?" he said.

Tetra had no response for him. Even though she could feel a little annoyance at his words, it was tempered by her feelings of empathy.

"We can follow the red trail," she said calmly.

"Into the darkness once more?" Tantalus jittered. "I can't go back there again. All those tweeth, all those…"

"It's OK," said Tetra. "Something feels different this time. Like this was the adventure I was supposed to go on all along."

She looked at the glowing harpoon and looked down at the red trail. She sighed and looked back at Tantalus.

"Shall we?" she said.

But before Tantalus could answer, the red trail divided, travelling in different directions. And there, from underneath them, a large black hole opened and encased them within. The whale had come back for more.

Chapter 22
Inside the Whale

It was damp. Some might even use the word moist, but for Tetra it was damp. Not quite like the aftermath of the particularly dreadful hurricanes that too frequently happened back home, but enough wetness that she could feel it, as opposed to how it felt in the sea where the water was much like the air on her skin. No, here it was damp.

It felt unusual to Tetra. She had been in the sea for so long and had wanted to leave it for as long as she had been there, but now she missed it. This place was sinister. It was dark, dreary and even more dreadfully damp than it had been a moment before. It was also humid, which made the damp even more damp.

"What's that smell?" came a recognisable voice.

"Tantalus!" Tetra cried. "Is that you?"

"You've taken me to some terwible places, but this might just be the worst," replied Tantalus.

Tetra ignored his sly joke. She was still clutching the harpoon which was still glowing a golden light, however much duller than it had been before. Like a torch in a cave, it guided her across the slippery, rubbery ground and towards Tantalus' voice.

"How do we get out of here?" she asked.

"Well, if I had any idea where this is going," said Tantalus. "It's going to get worse before it gets better. Then we get out and, just before I get to fill my belwy, we end up somewhere else."

"Look, over here," Tetra called over. She pulled the harpoon up to eye-height and shone its light across the section of the wall. There they could see large filament-like structures, much like the bristles on a brush, but much denser and much sharper.

"Here we go again," muttered Tantalus

"I know where we are!" said Tetra, turning around to face Tantalus. "We're inside the whale's mouth!"

A small noise came from the other side of the whale's mouth. It rustled, then once the rustling stopped, it squirmed, and when it squirmed, it let out a huge sigh. For all the big, scary creatures Tetra had encountered, this one didn't sound either big or scary. Indeed, it sounded quite small. And by quite small, it was definitely completely tiny.

"Who's there?" Tetra called out.

"Still just me," said Tantalus.

"Not you," snapped Tetra. "Can't you hear the rustling?"

"I assumed it was the tide through the whale's tweeth," said Tantalus.

"Not this time," said Tetra, as she shone the harpoon around the whale's mouth, following the rustle, and creeping carefully across the whale's rubbery tongue. And she had to be careful, the tongue wasn't steady but moved like any tongue would. But a 'tonguequake' was a mere inconvenience. Perhaps the most daunting aspect of all were the endless ridges and bumps that seemed to be tasting Tetra's skin.

"Oh, why me?" said a whisper from the direction of the rustles.

"Hello? Can you hear me?" Tetra called out to no reply. She continued her walk across the tongue, as perilous as it was. Even stranger was the realisation that this was the first time Tetra had walked since the day she was swept away. It felt strangely unnatural because her body had adjusted to the sea. Worryingly, she almost walked like an octopus would out of water, her ankles dragging and bending like tentacles, and her body flopping like jelly.

She reached the other side of the whale's mouth and noticed small movements in the bristling teeth. There, several legs poked out, as well as the bottom of a reddish shell. Tetra gently grabbed the shell with her finger and thumb and pulled the little creature free from the bristles.

"Oh, you again," said the voice.

"King Artemos!" exclaimed Tetra. "So, this is where you ended up."

"It seems the beast got us both," said the king. "Well, at least I can join my one true love in the next life."

"Not so soon," said Tetra. "I still think we can get out of here."

"You sure are brimming with golden confidence," said the shrimp.

"I think it's the harpoon," Tantalus called out from the other side of the mouth.

Of course, Tantalus was right. Before the harpoon, Tetra had been much more scared in the sea. But there was something comforting about the harpoon, something that made her feel everything was going to get better sooner rather than later. Unfortunately, the whale had other ideas.

Not long after King Artemos had been freed from the bristles, the whale began to stir. She started gritting her teeth and enough water flowed back into the mouth to lift Tantalus off his belly. Then with one almighty gulp, the whale washed a wave of water through her gigantic mouth, passing Tetra, Tantalus and King Artemos down her cavern and into an enormous pit.

Tetra was getting used to being in the dark. First it happened in the forest, then the upturned dinghy, then the ride on the whale down to the depths where the light can't reach. But the darkness she was in now was perhaps worst of all: the darkness of a whale's belly.

She stood up and lifted her harpoon up to catch her bearings. From her knees down, there was broken chitin (what the shells of certain creatures are made from) littering the stomach floor: the bones of the whale's dinner as Tantalus graciously put it. Or, for King Artemos, the bones of his once proud city.

Sadness seemed to drift in the air — or for whatever passed as air in the stomach of a whale. The atmosphere was dreary. The decomposing sludge underneath the chitin probably didn't help to brighten the mood, but even without the rotting flesh, Tetra could sense there was something else disturbing the whale here.

Tetra looked at Tantalus and then he looked back at her, then they both looked at King Artemos who happened to be staring at both of them. No one had words, and when words looked like they might escape from their mouths, only a sigh seemed to come from their lips. Amid the silence, the harpoon began uttering through Tetra's veins. It was mostly jibberish to her, but strangely, she knew what it meant, and began swimming through the chitin. Tantalus and King Artemos nervously followed.

A strange liquid leaked from the walls. It dripped on the chitin around them and sizzled like oil in a frying pan. Tantalus and King Artemos looked at each other with their mouths wide open, shaking as they followed Tetra — who seemed remarkably unfazed by the acidic lava dripping around them.

They passed a wooden barrel as they crawled through the lake of chitin. Then other wooden objects; namely a chair, pieces of table and many wooden spoons. It was a museum of sorts, one that showcased ancient and less ancient ship's furniture. At least in comparison with the captain's ship, the decor matched up.

The tattered rope that lingered around in chunks seemed to match that on the captain's ship. It frayed in the same way, snapped in the same way and even fluttered in the same way. But Tetra supposed, every ship could be made in the same way too.

There were whimpers echoing around the belly. Quiet whimpers. Subtle, but still shaking to the nerves.

"These cries," wept King Artemos. "They are the tears of the million shrimp."

"How do you know that?" asked Tantalus.

"When you've seen your subjects eaten by this beast, you know how they cry."

A white, whispery orb floated around near Tetra's head before vanishing into the chitin. Other orbs appeared and disappeared in the same way. The further they travelled through the chitin, the more seem to appear and disappear out of sight.

The whimpers became louder and by the time they reached the other side of the wall, the cries were a chorus. Tetra felt like they were guiding her somewhere. Even though she had reached the other end of the belly, she knew there was something more here. So, as the orbs fell one by one into the chitin, she began digging.

Not far below the surface, a small cage, as rusty as a lonely anchor, was submerged in the chitin. The acid made it slightly warm to touch, but with a little help from both Tantalus and King Artemos, they freed the cage from its lair.

Inside was another orb, a brighter orb, like the brightest star in the night sky. It seemed to be gazing not at Tetra, and definitely not at Tantalus, but at King Artemos. And with a fading glow, the orb slowly transformed into a shrimp.

"Hello, Artemos," said the ghostly shrimp.

"Eros!" cried King Artemos, sinking to his knees. "I'm so sorry."

"This isn't your fault," said Eros. "I don't even think it's the whale's fault. But you need to get out of here before you end up like me."

"I can't leave you again," cried Artemos. "Not now that I've found you again."

"It's too late for me," said Eros. "You must get out of here before it finds you."

"What finds us?" interrupted Tetra.

"The sea is dying," said Eros, turning to look back at Artemos. "My King, there are other shrimps still alive that need a king."

"They need two kings," cried Artemos.

"No, one will be more than enough."

There was a rumble underneath the chitin. The liquid was now streaming faster out of the walls like a burst pipe, soaking much of the chitin and dissolving it faster than Tantalus would a jellyfish. The chitin tumbled towards the walls as bones beneath them emerged from the depths.

It was a skeleton of sorts, much like the ones back on the ship, and it was wielding a scimitar and a ripped eyepatch. Tetra turned towards him, holding her harpoon in front of her.

Chapter 23
Too Little, Too Late

Tetra remembered her last encounter with a skeleton, it had been after all the captain's skeleton: strong and unwieldy, defiant in its lack of a brain, or more unnervingly, relentless in its pursuit. But for all his strength, it was just a bunch of bones. Bones fell apart when Tantalus came ploughing through him.

But perhaps it was Captain Neureus himself that was most unnerving. He had just sat there and watched as his former self came rampaging after her. This led her to a horrible thought: where was the ghost of this skeleton? Was he watching too? Or was this skeleton all alone in the belly of the beast?

The skeleton swung his scimitar towards Tetra and she jumped out of the way, crashing into the pile of chitin below. Her hair was caught in some of the rising acid and it sizzled on her head as she danced back to her feet.

She looked on, as the skeleton turned to face her once more, appearing to ignore both Tantalus and King Artemos, who was now safely hiding behind the other side of the cage. Its bony feet stumbled forward, his pelvis crunching against his thighs and its ribs already broken.

It grinned, showing several gold teeth still attached to an otherwise broken smile, then approached Tetra with the same menace as the captain's skeleton had before, a staggering determination to use its weapon once more.

Tantalus was flapping with his flippers, unable to show the

same agility as he would have had he still been in the sea. It turned out, the belly of a whale was a tricky place to be for a turtle, especially when there was a marauding skeleton approaching. He pushed through the chitin but could only muster a small nudge on the skeleton's foot, which the skeleton had barely noticed, and if it had, barely cared about.

Tetra raised her harpoon towards the skeleton; it now glowed with a purity that Tetra could feel through her veins. Its light reverberated across the stomach and, unlike any other light, it moved like water. It crashed against the walls like a wave, and flowed like a river towards distant horizons.

The skeleton swung its scimitar downwards towards Tetra's head. She lifted her harpoon with both hands and blocked its blade with the middle of the harpoon. His full weight kept pressing downwards and Tetra was using all her strength to keep the blade away from her.

From behind the skeleton, Tantalus started firing pieces of chitin at the skeleton with his flippers. They ricocheted off its bones but distracted the skeleton long enough for Tetra to push his scimitar away and launch a swipe of her own. Her harpoon slashed against the skeleton's ribs, knocking some of the loose ones off their perch.

"There's a large crack in the back of its skull," yelled Eros. "You need attack from behind."

Tantalus kept flinging loose chitin at the skeleton, hoping to distract it some more, but at this point, the skeleton seemed delirious. It was swinging its scimitar around in the gastric air, hitting nothing but its own arm in the process.

Tetra slid between its legs to get on the other side of it, and with one mighty jump, pushed the harpoon through the crack in the back of the skull. The skeleton bellowed and swung his scimitar around, flinging Tetra into the cage. She was bruised, but she had survived larger, more ferocious beasts in the sea than this skeleton. She rose to her feet and thrust her harpoon towards the skeleton.

It was, though, unnecessary. The skeleton suddenly staggered in the opposite direction; its skull falling open like a broken clam shell. After three steps, half of its skull snapped off and the skeleton fell to its knees. Once on its knees, the acid began to sizzle and dissolve its body, to which Tetra realised it was dangerously circling around them.

The cage was now all that was left between them and the acid. Tantalus lay on top, with Tetra on top of him and King Anteros on top of her. The acid sizzled on the bottom of the cage and it continued to rise.

"We need to save Eros!" cried King Anteros.

"Save me from what?" said Eros. "Can you not see? I am not of flesh and shell anymore. I am just a lost soul wandering the stomach of the whale, along with the other orbs you saw."

"That cannot be true," cried Anteros. "I can see you with my own eyes."

"You also just saw a skeleton which was very much dead," replied Eros. "No, my time in this world is over. But first, we must get you out of the stomach of the whale. Tetra, you must make the whale vomit."

"How do I do that?" said Tetra, her eyes watching the acid as it rose to Eros' first few legs.

"Use the harpoon on the stomach, it should be enough to upset the whale."

Tetra looked at her harpoon and then looked towards the belly. She then looked back down at the ever-rising acid which was now almost at Eros' head. She turned towards the belly, held the harpoon like a javelin and threw it towards the stomach lining.

The harpoon hit the belly and became firmly lodged in its lining. The stomach began to contract and the faint sound of the whale could be heard singing. Soon, the harpoon was pushed out of the hole it had made, but the stomach contracted so tight that it fired the cage, with Tetra, Tantalus and King Anteros on top, up into the air.

They flew into a narrow passage and soon found themselves shooting through the mouth and out of the whale. From there, they could see thousands, maybe even tens of thousands, of orbs leaving the whale's mouth and gathering around the trio.

King Eros arose from the now broken cage and approached King Anteros. And when King Eros approached, so did all the orbs, which all slowly took the form of shrimp. They bowed towards the kings with their heads facing the sand.

"It's time for us to leave," said King Eros, looking around at all the other shrimp. "Thanks for setting us free, my King."

King Anteros' eyes welled up. In the frozen landscape of the northern sea, his tears turned to icicles and then dropped like snow would on a breezy day. His tears followed the tide towards the horizon, which glowed for a new day.

As the sun began to peek over the horizon, the shrimps followed King Eros, swimming the path made by Anteros' tears. And as the sunlight blossomed from a pink to yellow, the souls of a once proud city were too far for eyes to see, too far for ears to hear, but not too far for Anteros to feel. It was then that he smiled.

The whale by now had caught her breath and seemed unsure of her next move. Tetra's harpoon lay near the broken cage, half-sunk into the sand. She pulled it out of its bed, but the harpoon no longer glowed, nor could Tetra hear it talk anymore, it seemed just like a regular harpoon.

"Boreas, they call her," said King Anteros. "The beast of the northern sea, destroyer of my kingdom, the demon no doubt of many kingdoms."

"The whale was a victim just as much as we were," said Tetra. "I believe this harpoon was somehow both the cause and the solution to her problems."

"A weapon like that probably takes on the heart of the one that holds it," said the king. "At least for now Boreas won't want to eat."

One half of an iceberg bounced in front of them, trying endlessly to escape the barrier that either kept everyone in or kept something out. Boreas nodded her head, and slowly moved over to the glacier. She nudged it gently — at least gently for her — to reveal millions of small eggs underneath.

"The birth of a new kingdom," the king gasped. He looked at the whale with his jaw wide open, then looked back at the iceberg before swimming beneath it. "So many future subjects and so little time."

"Or future dinner for the whale," muttered Tantalus, to which Tetra elbowed him in the chest and gave him a stern frown.

"I think I know what I need to do," said the king. "I shall create a new city in the name of Eros," and he immediately began tending the eggs.

"I guess this is goodbye then," said Tetra, cautiously approaching the bottom of the iceberg.

"It appears so," said the king, turning towards her. "Thank you for all your help. I'd have never seen Eros again if it hadn't been for you."

"I'm sure we can find some more whales to get…" Tantalus said before having another elbow launched into his rib. "I mean, no pwoblem at all," he stumbled.

"Feel free to take any ice you need from the old city," said the king. "I will be building a new one right here, with even bigger walls!"

"That's great," said Tetra, "but I have another plan."

****

The other half of the iceberg wasn't too far away. It didn't take long on the back of a whale to reach it, nor did it take long for the whale to drag it to the coral reef, where an impatient Hermes was al-ready waiting on top of one of the white shards.

"Took your time, didn't you," said Hermes, still stumbling around with the captain's hat. "I almost sold this hat for a wellington boot."

"We're glad you didn't," said Tetra, as Boreas hauled in the ice cube, which instantly began to melt.

"Quite the beast you found there," said Hermes. "I bet she could haul my whole shop around the sea."

The iceberg soon melted, and the coral reef went from hot to warm. Hermes lay back in bliss, snug on his coral perch. He then lifted the hat and pushed it towards Tetra. It floated slowly until it reached her hands.

"Thanks for your help," he said. "I'm sure the coral reef will be teeming with new customers by tomorrow."

"That's OK," said Tetra. "It was nice to meet you."

"As to you... I best be off to prepare my store. See you soon."

With that, the crab snuck beneath the broken coral until he could be seen no more. Boreas had headed back to the colder seas, leaving Tetra and Tantalus to go back to the ship on their own.

Chapter 24
Walking the Plank

The ship sat slightly higher in the water; not floating, but certainly closer to the surface than it had been before. The sails fluttered against the sea's breeze, only held in place by a giant anchor stuck between some rocks and the yellow-tinged sand. It was an interesting anchor, not because of its enormous size but because its shape resembled a squid, with some of the tentacles as sharp as the harpoon that Tetra carried.

They drifted across the deck like an eel would nervously leave its burrow. Tetra felt glaring eyes down her spine and the harpoon felt cold as its once golden light turned a misty blue. The crew seemed even more menacing than before. At the very least, they seemed displeased by a young girl and turtle on their newly repaired ship.

Captain Nereus stood outside his cabin's door, his eyes a gleaming red above a gnawing grin. He walked slowly away from his cabin and down the stairs until he was a mere two feet away from Tetra, then raised his arms towards his crew.

"The girl has delivered!" he exclaimed. "Now it is time to release her from her duty."

Crowds of laughter filled the sea, and it echoed back several times, each echo a more sinister tone than the one before.

"Now can you take me home?" asked Tetra, her eyes fixed on the captain's.

"Most certainly," replied the captain. "At least, perhaps, closer to home than you were before."

The crew grew rowdier. With every grain of sand that flickered by in the sea, the darkness in their eyes seemed to grow more sombre. Their eyes absorbed any light that the harpoon had left, leaving a darkness that wasn't only the absence of light, but the enemy of light.

Tetra passed the hat over to the captain and reminded him once more of his promise: to get her home, back to the island which she had never thought she would miss. In Tetra's heart, she knew she might always dream of adventures; at least, adventures without her being at the bottom of the food chain. But she now knew, it doesn't matter where the journey goes and what road it might take, the adventure always leads back home.

"Are you forgetting something?" said the captain, holding his other hand out.

"Oh, the harpoon?" said Tetra.

The captain's eyes grew more intense as he stretched his hand out further, his grin slowly becoming more of a grimace as the seconds went by.

Tetra cautiously moved the harpoon towards the captain's hand. And without much delay, he snatched it from her and smiled once more.

"It can be quite the attachment, can't it?" he said. "A weapon like this is way too much for a little girl. May I recommend a spoon next time?" he sneered, to even more laughter from his crew.

The captain then adjusted his hat, looked towards his crew and walked back up the stairs. When he reached the top, he looked down at both Tetra and Tantalus and licked his lips. The harpoon was now shining a dark light that jittered around the ship like a nervous goldfish trapped in a bowl. Tetra could feel the pain of the harpoon as it whimpered in the clutches of the captain, but it was too late now, it was time for her to go home.

"Make our guests comfy," snarled the captain, pointing the harpoon towards a cage.

Before Tetra and Tantalus had time to react, her hands and his flippers were grabbed by the crew. Tantalus was dragged into a rusty cage that was hauled high up onto the mast with a large chain. As for Tetra, she found herself bound by rope, tied up so tight she could barely speak.

"You lied," she murmured, trying to scream without success.

"Have you learnt nothing about the sea since you've been here?" asked the captain, as he opened his cabin door. "There's no such things as lies down here, only... open promises."

A loud scraping noises could be heard coming from behind the captain's door. Seconds later, his skeleton appeared, dragging a large sword behind him. He looked bigger than he had been before and, if not taller, certainly mightier.

The crew chanted and raised their own weapons, a collection of rusty daggers, broken harpoons, and even weaponry best used on a kitchen table. The captain's skeleton dropped his sword which in turn clunked down the steps until it was on the deck in front of the crew and a fight broke out until one lucky pirate claimed the sword as his own.

Captain Neureus faced his skeleton and smirked. It was the kind of smirk that turned the sea colder and the world a little darker. Even the tide itself seemed afraid and decided to go towards the other horizon. And the moon was hesitant to glow, but when it did so, it was a blood red rather than its usually pearly self.

"It's time we avenged our own death," said the captain to his skeleton. He put the hat on top of the skeleton's head and held out the harpoon towards his bony self. The right hand of the skeleton reached out and grasped the harpoon, sending a dark pulse throughout the ship. His left hand then grasped it too and he lifted it towards his ribs.

Captain Neureus faced his crew and nodded with a huge grin. He then faced the skeleton and looked deep into the holes on his face. He walked forward until his ghostly body was standing where the skeleton was standing and turned around to face the crew once more. Dark light spilt from the harpoon and the red light from the moon was sent weeping back from the sea. His wispy hands joined with the bony hands of the skeleton, and where the skeleton once had two holes, it now had two eyes.

"Well, isn't this unusual?" said the captain, admiring his skeletal body. "I'm almost as good looking as I was before."

Tetra could only watch. She couldn't resist the rope she was bound by, nor could she wiggle away from the braying pirates. She looked up and saw the captain was now standing right above her, his skeleton now back in his full control.

"So you wanted to go home?" said the captain in a grimacing tone. "But where is home? That island you were once so eager to get away from? No, that can't be home. Why would you want to go back somewhere you disliked so much?"

The crew moved away as the captain began to walk around the deck, still admiring the angry light coming from his harpoon. He stopped by the cage that held Tantalus and chattered his teeth, finishing with the sound of a lick of a tongue.

"And what about this turtle? When was the last time we had dinner, lads?"

The once chanting crew were now a zealous mob, elated to eat what their bodies had once tasted before. Tantalus hid behind his flippers and appeared to be murmuring unintelligibly. But, for a brief moment, Tetra could have sworn she heard the turtle say 'he wasn't a jellyfish'. Her head sunk towards the deck and she became motionless as the loud steps of the captain approached her once more.

"Time to take her home, lads!" he roared to his crew. "Then

next stop, we have our revenge! To the Kraken!"

Two pirates lifted her up and walked towards the side of the ship. There was a short plank laid out over its side, shoddily built together by scrap wood, some of it buckling under the wispy feet of the two ghouls. With her hands tied with rope, and heavy rocks tied to her feet, she was prodded along the plank.

As she stared back towards the crew, the captain stood above them, with the harpoon glowing darker by the second. And before she could say any last words, the plank snapped, and the weights around her feet carried downwards.

As she fell, Tetra saw the ship start to slowly move away from her. Darkness flooded into her eyes, and the entire world, except for the ship, disappeared. She watched the ship sail away slowly through the darkness, illuminated by its own dark light that scared away all other light. It moved in the direction of the coral reef, cutting through the sea like a rusty submarine. And when it was just a speck in the distance, her back thudded against the sand below. She shut her eyes, awaiting the death she knew had stalked her throughout this adventure. In the darkness of her own mind, she thought where she had been and who she had met. But it seemed all thoughts brought her back to the turtle she had met. The turtle that never left her even when she had wanted him to. And the turtle that had stayed when she needed someone most.

She fell asleep inside a tsunami of thoughts. Even as her body rested, her mind couldn't. She could feel the force of the tsunami on her body once more. She felt like a fish in a bowl, or worse of all, a shrimp trapped in a bottle.

Chapter 25
The Crack in the Barrier

Light glared across Tetra's eyes like a flame chasing dynamite. Her right eye opened before her left, and when her left eye did eventually open, her hands covered her sight to avoid the intensity. She slowly took her hands away to gather her bearings, but as it turned out, her bearings were no good here. To be here was to be somewhere different.

The water was warm. It almost felt like it was cuddling her. For the first time, Tetra sensed the sea wasn't resisting her, or as it had in the past, trying to rip her limb from limb. It was to Tetra quite a pleasant feeling. A feeling she hadn't felt in quite some time.

And when her eyes adjusted to the light, what she saw was even more pleasant. She lay on white, crystal sand which tumbled gently through the joyful blue sea like a fluffy cloud would in the sky. Small, pink shrubs grew in pockets where small fish slept the day away in harmony. Was it a lagoon where Tetra could forget all her problems and live in the moment? A destination worth the journey she had been on, perhaps?

Tetra lay back and enjoyed the sun. From the frozen sea where the whale lived, to the dark forests where the Hydra had appeared, this lagoon was for sure the best place she had been. She closed her eyes and sighed in relief, enjoying her well-deserved rest. It was, however, to be short-lived.

Tetra's mind started to oppose her body. While her back slowly sunk into the sand like she was back home in her bed, her thoughts began talking. And when their whispers were ignored, they spoke louder, and when that was ignored, they showed her visions of the world before the lagoon: the ship, the pirates, the turtle.

She sat up and let the current flow gently through her hair. In that instant, she saw a small turtle, maybe a recent hatchling, nudging a clam around with its beak. He appeared to be giggling, like Tantalus, but probably centuries younger.

Not far from the small turtle was a small dolphin, clapping his flippers in the direction of the small turtle. The turtle nudged the clam towards the dolphin and then the dolphin nudged it back to the turtle. They both started giggling.

As she looked around, she noticed more creatures enjoying themselves. A group of baby seahorses zoomed past, closely followed by their father. A large dugong was lounging amongst the pink flowers, scratching its behind with its flipper. Even the crabs seemed to be trading shells without too much bickering.

While gazing around the beautiful lagoon, something dropped onto her lap. She peered down to see a clam resting peacefully on her thigh. She looked back up to see a small dolphin and a small turtle looking towards her.

The dolphin nudged the turtle forward. The turtle, with his face down, slowly drifted until he was just in front of Tetra.

"'Cuse me, Miss Mermaid," the young turtle stuttered. "Can we have our ball back?"

"Of course," said Tetra, throwing it gently towards the turtle.

"Thanks, miss," he said, as he nudged the clam towards the dolphin and paddled away, giggling once more.

They were having fun, much more than Tetra had ever had. She thought of school and wondered if she really did have any friends, then realised she didn't. Not one that she could really call a friend.

The harsher truth was, once she was away from school, she was alone. And perhaps worst of all, she was lonely. She had been lonely then and she was lonely now.

She smiled as she watched at the turtle and the dolphin playing. She began to realise that her only true friend had been Tantalus all along. The adventure wasn't where you were going but how you got there. And maybe, just maybe, she had had a little fun.

She watched on as the turtle nudged the shell towards the dolphin, who spun around and whacked it with his tail. The clam flew through the sea like a bullet, rising higher and higher until it hit the barrier. Only, it didn't come back down.

The turtle and the dolphin stared up from beneath where the clam had struck the barrier. Tetra swam over and looked up towards the barrier, and there, wedged inside it was the clam.

"How is that possible?" said the turtle.

"We can't get it back," said the dolphin. "It'll zap us."

"Let me try," said Tetra, swimming towards the barrier.

"Be careful," said the turtle. "The zap will hurt your fwipper."

Tetra gently paddled towards the surface, and once there, she noticed something peculiar. There was a small crack, only large enough for the edge of a clam to wedge itself tight into.

She pushed her fingers close to the clam, being as careful as she could. Her fingers brushed against the clam and she began to clench them until she had a small grip. She pulled gently, but it didn't budge. She then pulled harder, and her finger scraped the barrier, receiving a zap.

"Owch!"

"Told you," came a voice from below. Tetra frowned, tried once more, and got the same result.

"Watch your fwipper," came the voice once more.

"I can't pull it out," said Tetra, floating close to it with her hands on her hips.

"We could find another clam," said the dolphin.

"But this is my favouwite cwam," said the turtle.

"We will get your clam," said Tetra. "I'm just curious about how the barrier has cracked. Did the clam crack it or was it cracked to begin with?"

Before she could think too much about the crack in the barrier, a stream of bubbles punched their way through the water inches behind her and hit the clam. The clam rattled and jiggled until it fell from the crack and sunk back down to the ground.

"Yay!" said the turtle.

"Thank you, Miss Seahorse," said the dolphin.

Tetra turned around to see a large seahorse blowing bubbles in the same way Bubbles had done. In fact, this seahorse was so much like Bubbles that it was even zooming circles around Tetra like the small seahorse had.

"Is that you, Bubbles?" asked Tetra, with her mouth falling open in surprise.

The seahorse appeared to nod, then blew more bubbles towards Tetra, before whizzing around erratically.

"That is you, Bubbles!" said Tetra, beaming a smile from ear to ear.

Bubbles threw Tetra onto her back and rode her around at lightning speed. This time, it wasn't the turtle giggling, nor was it the dolphin giggling, but it was Tetra. She was having fun. More fun than she had ever had.

The problem was, having fun only reminded her of Tantalus.

"Bubbles?" said Tetra, in a quiet voice. The seahorse stopped playing and halted just above some pink flowers. "I lost Tantalus."

Bubbles snorted, brewing a disjointed bubble into the water.

"I think I know where he might be, but it is somewhere very dangerous."

There was a moment of silence. Even the sea briefly stopped moving; the tide quit its adventure towards the horizon and current forgot where it was flowing to. Then, out of nowhere, Bubbles spiralled in circles with Tetra still on her back, and then growled towards the horizon.

"Does that mean you're coming?" asked Tetra.

Bubbles, without a moment's hesitation, nodded and started blowing bubbles that crackled on the barrier above.

"Do you know where the Kraken lives?" asked Tetra. "That's where I think he might be."

Bubbles glanced in different directions, towards several different horizons, before nodding in the direction of the coral reef.

"That way?" asked Tetra, to which Bubbles nodded once more and began to trot through the pink flowers and towards the white walls.

You weaving?" came a voice nearby. Tetra turned to see the turtle and the dolphin looking up at them.

"We must go to find my friend," said Tetra. "He's a turtle just like you."

"You mean there are other twurtles?" he replied with a massive smile. "I thought I was the only one! Did you hear that?"

"Are there other dolphins too?" asked the dolphin.

"I am sure there are," smiled Tetra, her eyes now a warm scarlet, as the sunset reflected in her gaze. "We must go now," said Tetra. "I hope we meet again. Maybe next time I can play too."

"Of course," smiled the turtle, waving his flipper as Bubbles began to trot towards the horizon.

It had been a long day: there was no doubt about it as the sun set as slow as a sea slug sliding down a rock. It had also been a great day. but it had not been, as she had thought, the end of her journey. Tetra's adventure was only just beginning to unfold.

Chapter 26
The Dark before the Darkness

The sea, as great and vast as it was, felt much smaller on the back of a large seahorse. What would have taken Tetra hours took Bubbles minutes. He galloped like the ocean was merely a small meadow, with mountains merely hills and forests merely trees.

It wasn't long before Tetra could see the white walls of the coral reef, all the more bleached and looking all the more broken. It may have been lifeless before, but now it felt like a different planet; Mars would have felt comparatively teeming with life. But, at the very least, it was familiar. And for all the creatures Tetra had visited under the sea, an annoying crab had been the most welcoming.

"Hermes!" Tetra called out. "Are you home?"

There was no answer, not even the rattling of eight little legs or the bobbling of a tin or a saucepan, just snorts from Bubbles' nose and his tail brushing the tip of the sand.

"Where is he?" Tetra asked, to which Bubbles could only snort in reply.

They rode through the crumbling white walls of coral and the rocks of sponges that lay around like an undersea graveyard. Whatever the ice cube was supposed to do, it hadn't done, or at least not enough to save the reef from the ever-warming sun.

Not far away, a small structure built from broken coral stood abandoned. It had a sign made from driftwood which said 'Hermes' Homes'. All around the structure were broken shells of various shapes and colours.

"It looks like his shop didn't make it," sighed Tetra.

"This little light of mine, I'm gonna let it shine."

"I recognise that voice!" said Tetra, flicking her head around in different directions. Bubbles jumped to face the other way and in the distance near the horizon, a dim light could be seen drifting closer.

"This little light of mine, I'm gonna let it shine."

"That must be Apollo!" said Tetra, edging Bubbles to move closer to the light, to which he did without fuss or hesitation. And, indeed, it was the little anglerfish from before. They had met briefly in the lands of the worm beasts, before they had gone in different directions.

"Apollo!" Tetra called out, but there was no reply at first. The anglerfish seemed lost his own world, singing his song as he approached the white walls. "Apollo!" she shouted once more, at which his little head popped out and his needle teeth poked from his mouth.

"Tetra!" said Apollo. "How could I forget such a strange creature."

"Did you find the forest?" asked Tetra.

"Well, I found what was left of it," he said. "I came up from the deep expecting lush green forests and lively colours, and all I got were the fading embers cooling in the burning waters."

"I did warn you."

"That you did. I guess your trip to the coral reef didn't work out either? This actually looks worse than before."

"Yes," Tetra agreed, sadly. "But I'm looking for friend Hermes. He used to live here."

"Probably moved north like the rest of the creatures. I saw swarms of different creatures heading to the colder waters only a few days ago."

"I guess that's to be expected," Tetra sighed, looking around once more at the deserted graveyard that the coral reef had become.

"What happened to your turtle friend?" asked Apollo. "Did he go north too?"

"No," Tetra sighed, with her head sinking into her shoulders. "He was captured by some pirates and I think they were heading towards the Kraken."

"The Kraken? Why, that's where I'm going! She lives in the deep which happens to be my home too!"

"You live near the Kraken?"

"Sure, she's not so bad when you get used to her. Come, follow me, you can accompany me home."

****

Apollo led them east, past the crumbling white walls and through empty sand dunes, drifting between small mountains and large hills. Fish, some in small schools and others in large shoals, pushed past them in the other direction, no doubt heading north to the cooler waters.

Above, large plastic bags, as big and as delicate as the jelly beasts, gently swam in the same direction as Tetra and Apollo: towards the deep. They bobbled against the barrier, which repelled them down about halfway towards the seabed, and then they floated back up only to repeat the cycle. It occurred to Tetra that they probably were the jelly beasts, or at least they had been the jelly beasts. From gentle mushrooms in the forest to ferocious plastic bags in the deep, their transition was complete.

"This little light of mine, I'm gonna let it shine."

To Apollo, nothing that was happening seemed to faze him. The giant plastic bags seemed to go unnoticed and the shoals of fish moving in the opposite direction didn't seem to herald any questions. He just continued singing his song until the seabed began to slope downwards gradually.

"Almost there now," said Apollo. "The sea will soon become darker and my little light will lead the way."

The sand tumbled slowly down the slope, as did small rocks and pieces of litter. The slope wasn't steep, however, and fortunately being undersea meant it didn't really matter. Bubbles was a swift seahorse, able to swim in a multitude of directions at ease. As for Apollo, well, he looked relatively unapproachable anyway. Even the rocks avoided him.

Small holes appeared in the sand and Tetra instantly recognised them. The worm beasts were about and they must have been hungry. They popped out at even the sound of the rocks and when it wasn't a fish, they pulled back, dejected, into their holes hoping a meal would slip by soon.

But every meal had long gone north at this point. The sea here was barren, more barren than the coral reef had been, and that was more barren than the desert had been. Perhaps the whole sea now had become a desert, Tetra thought. Besides the lagoon, of course, that seemed like a world within another world.

The sand below was slowly becoming more and more steep. In the distance, the sand could be seen flowing above a deep, dark trench, like a river of sand flowing into the sunset. The holes beneath them were getting bigger; one was about a metre in length. Luckily, nothing appeared from it, but it had Bubbles snorting nervously.

They paddled through, almost creeping. Apollo's light appeared to be flickering like a busted streetlight, and his song had become much quieter than it had been before. There was a sudden sharp drop of about two metres that seemed to curve slightly.

The sand swirled around like a slow-moving whirlpool. It was sinking slowly in the centre but rising sharply around the edges.

Tetra looked down and, where the sand was sinking, she spotted big, sharp teeth hiding beneath.

"We need to get out of here!" she yelled, pulling Bubbles to turn around. And he was quick, he galloped to the edge as Tetra grabbed onto one of Apollo's fins. By the time they made it out of the hole, a giant worm beast rose as high as the barrier and stared back down at them.

He screeched a deafening scream. It was as high-pitched as a boiling kettle and as loud as the song of a whale. Before they could move a few steps away from the hole, the giant worm beast grabbed a plastic bag from out of the ocean sky and recoiled back into its lair.

Tetra rode Bubbles upwards slightly and found many large craters. Craters that no doubt harboured many giant worm beasts. It was a minefield of teeth, ready to explode the moment they hesitated over one for too long. Apollo shrugged and reassured Tetra that he came this route a lot. But something must have changed, he concurred, before gently singing his song once more as they edged their way around the minefield.

The swarm of plastic bags continued to float above and, every so often, a worm beast would rise from its lair and snatch one or two. There were so many plastic bags at this point that it didn't seem to matter. They continued to float above before sinking down a dark chasm in the distance.

"The trench," said Apollo. "We are almost there."

And indeed they were. Having found a quiet route without worm beasts, they crept towards the trench's edge, where the slope became more of a drop, and the blue below became a deep black.

"Home," sighed Apollo. "You honestly miss it when you're away too long."

"I've come to realise that myself," sighed Tetra.

"Maybe this can be your home too."

"I'm not sure it has exactly what I need," replied Tetra.

"It has everything a fish could want," said Apollo. "Tasty food that literally walks into your mouth. No need for chasing it."

"Sounds more like the perfect place for Tantalus." She sighed once more. "Let's go find that silly turtle and bring him home."

They sunk slowly down into the darkness. And when the sun went dim, Apollo's light became bright. But it wasn't the only light, there were many lights just like his, bobbling around just like he did.

Chapter 27
The Crack in the Sea

Small rocks tumbled from above. The current carried them for as long as it could before dropping them down the trench where they disappeared into the darkness. Always the darkness survived. It smothered the trench from the top unto its bottom. Even the cliffs on its edges were concealed by a dark veil that could only be revealed by touch or by the fortune of Apollo's lamp.

And it was the light from Apollo that kept the real darkness away. Sometimes, darkness isn't the absence of light but the enemy of light, and what hides in the enemy of light are the strangest of beasts.

Tetra rode Bubbles as close to Apollo as she could, his lamp flickering through the sea like a lighthouse through a storm; a hurricane was waiting. Other lights that flickered had their own sets of teeth, and unlike Apollo, they didn't seem too friendly.

One such beast tried to snap at Bubbles' tail, only for Apollo to scare it away with a strong light, revealing a beast as long as the electric beast, but with larger teeth and a pale complexion. There were others, each with their own set of teeth, each scared away by Apollo's light.

The darkness, though, had its own ideas. It smothered Apollo's light like a blanket, and like a needle, the light ravelled its way through each strand of darkness. The light was delicate. Once it hit a wall or another creature, it broke.

And when it broke, the creatures slithered closer.

Then the lamp would strike back with more light and they slithered away.

There seemed to be a deep hunger in the darkness. Everyone was out to eat everyone, only they didn't want to get caught doing it. The deeper they travelled, the thicker the flow of the darkness, and the larger the teeth that stared back at them. Without her harpoon, Tetra had been starting to feel helpless. But she wouldn't show it, at least not to discourage Bubbles.

They travelled deeper into the darkness, so deep that Tetra could feel the weight of the water above her. Bubbles was tiring, but he continued without hesitation. But Tetra soon noticed he had stopped blowing bubbles, or if he hadn't, they were popping before they left his nose. The great weight of the sea was a buckling force.

They reached a ledge that was at least a mile across. On the east side of it the trench continued to go deeper. There were small vents on the ledge where the water was significantly warmer. Small, translucent worms gathered around these vents, only moving when a small lava plume dripped from it. The water fizzled around the lava before the lava itself was turned to stone, before rolling down the east-side cliff.

For Apollo, though, this was merely his back garden. Or, at the very least, his local neighbourhood. The lava plume might have amazed both Tetra and Tantalus, but what tickled Apollo's belly were the worms around the vent. He dangled his light towards them and one of the worms began swimming towards it. Before Tetra could ask what he was doing, the worm found itself in his mouth, never to be seen again.

"You miss your wossname... home comforts when you're away," said Apollo. "Especially the local cuisine. I just couldn't find worms like this up by the surface."

"That doesn't look too nice," cringed Tetra.

"Each to their own," said Apollo. "I personally can't get

enough of them, and the best part of it all, they just swim into your mouth!"

"I prefer food that doesn't move," said Tetra, screwing up her nose.

"I've never met a food that doesn't move," said Apollo.

Apollo made his way down the eastern ledge, closely followed by Tetra on the back of Bubbles. They followed the lava stones that dropped down into a never-ending darkness. There were more ledges with more vents, more lava that cooled to form more ledges, which in turn created more vents. An endless cycle of vents creating ledges and ledges creating vents. And it was hot, much hotter than before. Tetra and Bubbles certainly felt it, but Apollo seemed unconcerned.

Further down, bent and twisted pieces of wood were rising up around them, which had been scorched by the lava and turned into charcoal. A piece of cloth laid snagged on a sharp rock, then in a blink of an eye, was sizzled by a small lava trickle that crawled across the ledge to reach it. The deeper they went, the more remnants of wood and cloth they would find, even more twisted and bruised out of shape.

"The wossname... Kraken has feasted recently," chuckled Apollo. "Always a feast down here."

"It looks like pieces of the captain's ship," said Tetra, looking around at the debris. "Look, there's the flag with the castle on it!" She pointed towards a piece of fabric hooked onto a sharp piece of rock. There it stood, the captain's flag, less majestic as it was before.

Apollo glanced an eye towards Tetra then carried on down the 'ladder' into the darkness. The streams of lava were now joining into larger streams that didn't cool quite so quickly. Soon, the larger streams flowed into a river which trickled a 'lavafall' down into the darkness.

"The wossname... The Great Crack," said Apollo. "This is

about as far as I can go. You will need to follow the lavafall down into the darkness. The wossname... Kraken doesn't live far from here."

"What will we do without your light?" asked Tetra, looking around at the glimmers of light that had teeth attached to them.

"My larger friends won't come near you if you stay close to the lava. It'll be hot, but you'll be fine. There's a pool of lava at the bottom, and not far from there, there's another large hole where the Kraken lives."

"Where will you go?"

"My family isn't far from here; I shall see them and tell them stories of the wossname... shallow waters above. It wasn't the adventure I expected."

"Neither was mine," Tetra mumbled, looking towards the lava falling into an endless abyss. "But I guess the adventure isn't where you go, but who you meet on the way," Tetra said with a smile.

"That's something I never considered," said Apollo. "I guess you made some good friends, especially wossname... the turtle."

Apollo drifted a few metres away and looked towards the other end of the abyss, and then turned to look back at Tetra with what appeared to be a smile, but Tetra couldn't be sure with his large fangs always hanging out his mouth.

"Go find your turtle, I will tell my family I had the greatest adventure of all. I found new friends."

They embraced briefly, as well as a human and an anglerfish could embrace. It was more Tetra doing the embracing and Apollo existing. But it happened.

And after it had happened, Apollo nodded and moved his way above the abyss, to which the lavafall flowed into the darkness. In a few seconds, all that could be seen was his flicking lamp.

"Well, this is our moment," said Tetra, stroking the mane of Bubbles. "This is our time to shine brightly. Let's go save

Tantalus."

Shrieks from the darkness echoed through the abyss. Whatever was down there was staying away from the lavafall, which Bubbles and Tetra followed from a generous distance.

The heat was unbearable, and the steam clouded the vision. The only way Tetra knew that she was drifting too close to the lava was due to the sudden intensity of the heat. It did feel much safer than what awaited them in the darkness though.

It took maybe thirty minutes, probably longer, but soon they arrived at a large pool of lava. The lavafall crashed into it with great power, causing huge waves of lava that tumbled onto the shore. Fortunately, the shore was vast, and the lava eventually cooled around the lava pool's edges.

They arrived at a huge opening, like two giant rooms joined together by a broken wall. Inside the gap, a large tentacle laid dormant. It had suckers the size of small boats and a purple complexion that was smothered in a mist of darkness.

Tetra rode Bubbles slowly towards the giant tentacle before it slithered away from them and fell down a cliffside.

They approached the cliff edge and looked around. The hole was bigger than the last hole, much bigger. While the other looked like a meteorite had crashed into the surface, this one looked like a planet had collided with another.

Another tentacle wandered in the distance before falling back into the darkness. It was so big that it made Tetra gulp and then shudder. She patted Bubbles' mane once more and began to guide her down into the abyss.

Tetra knew what awaited her, but it didn't make it any more predictable.

Chapter 28
The Black Hole of the Sea

Legend had it, the island itself, the one that Tetra called home, was created by a Kraken. Or a continent was broken by a Kraken and made into many islands. Each island a surviving pillar that hadn't been pulled into the darkness of the sea.

Tetra didn't think that was likely. Astronauts had been to the moon, spaceships had visited Mars, and going back in time, meteorites had destroyed the dinosaurs. But anything other than plate tectonics creating islands didn't seem logical. But what was logical anymore? What was rational? Had this adventure not changed her perception?

Her reality had certainly changed. She was no longer bored on an island, but instead chasing a giant octopus down in the dark abyss. She knew she had to return to the island; however, it was the least of her worries right then. Tantalus needed her and to some extent, she felt she needed Tantalus.

The stars in the sky had long disappeared but new stars flickered around in the darkness of the abyss. These stars had teeth attached to them though, and while that would usually be a problem, they seemed to be staying away for now.

Tetra rode Bubbles slowly down into the darkness. And dark it remained. The tentacles had concealed themselves in the depth of the mist, and the water itself was increasingly feeling oily.

"I feel this is it, Bubbles," Tetra whispered, stroking the

seahorse's neck. "Somewhere down here we will find Tantalus." She paused to look around at the cloud of darkness and the small rocks tumbling down the cliff edge. "Hopefully alive," she whispered.

A loud impact rumbled below them, and the sound of rocks falling followed soon after. They paused briefly; the lights of other creatures flickered above them. The water was beginning to move more excitedly as Bubbles struggled to withstand its power.

The lights that flickered were soon stretching into short lines, and a strange sludge began to rise and cling to Tetra's fingers. Bubbles was now unable to control his movements and the water was pulling them downwards like the plug in a bath had been pulled out.

In front of Tetra, a large eye appeared. Large perhaps wasn't the word. Maybe massive. It was as big as a whale was wide, and it stared without a single blink.

Bubbles tried to pull away from it but she couldn't, she was trapped in the vortex of what felt like a black hole. Tetra stared back into the eye and gritted her teeth. She felt she had been here before. Perhaps it was the hydra, or the shark, or maybe even the whale, but here she had been.

The eye disappeared back into the darkness and the speed of the water increased as they descended further into the abyss.

"Hold tight, Bubbles," said Tetra, reassuring her with a stroke on the neck. "I think we're about to meet the Kraken."

In the corner of Tetra's left eye, a tentacle rose a few metres away from them. Its large suckers were quelching in the oily water, and a dark mist seemed to silently surround its purple complexion.

"Remember how strong you've become," Tetra said to Bubbles, her eyes fixed on the tentacle. "Now is the time to fight this current with all your might."

Bubbles snorted and an oily bubble rose from his snout and

popped not long after leaving. Her eyes focused on the tentacle in front as she started to swim against the current. Tetra held on tight as Bubbles forged ahead with all her might.

The current was still pulling them down, but they were slowing. But slowing wouldn't be enough. Slowing down only meant getting to the same place just later. But then that stopped being the problem entirely.

Now the tentacle was stirring and began moving towards them. Tetra gasped and in a split second, Bubbles did what Bubbles naturally did: she blew bubbles.

Only, she blew them in a stream, just like she had done when she knocked the clam out of the barrier. This time though, the stream hit harder and faster, pushing both her and Tetra away from the pursuing tentacle.

"You did it!" Tetra exclaimed with a huge smile on her face.

The smile was short-lived though. Now there were two tentacles. One in front of her and another behind. She gulped and patted Bubbles on the shoulder once more.

"The Kraken won't give up easily," she whispered. "It's time for even more bubbles."

Bubbles pushed out her chest and trumpeted a flow that ricocheted against the cliffs, causing rocks to fall into the abyss. Her eyes narrowed as she stared towards the first tentacle in front of her. She then began trotting towards it.

It didn't take long for Bubbles to pick up speed, and within seconds, a trot became a gallop. She whizzed towards the first tentacle at lightning speed, using the current to pick up even more speed. The other tentacle was chasing close behind.

As she became within a metre of the first tentacle, she blew a great stream of bubbles that bounced off it. It propelled them around it, like a comet dancing around a star, and pushed them behind the tentacle.

Moments later, a huge wave of water hit them as the two tentacles collided. A loud shriek came from below them as the two tentacles sunk back into the abyss.

There was silence. It was so silent that even the water stopped moving. Not even the lights moved anymore. Not even a single flicker.

"Is that it?" said Tetra, looking around into the darkness. "It can't be, there's still no Tantalus."

There was a sudden rumble below them. Rocks began to fall from the skies at great speed. The lights around them had all but disappeared.

"We need to move fast!" said Tetra. "Swim up!"

Bubbles puffed up her chest and galloped as fast as she could towards the top of the dark abyss. Rocks continued to fall as Bubbles dodged each one with incredibly agility. She was fast, but as Tetra looked behind her, several tentacles were coming up behind them with even greater speed.

"The tentacles are coming!" yelled Tetra, as Bubbles continued dodging the rocks.

The rocks were slowing Bubbles down and, to make matters worse, they did nothing to the tentacles. The tentacles were too big, too quick, too strong. The rocks merely crumbled in their path, turning to small clouds of sand that slowly sunk into the darkness.

Four tentacles were soon level with Tetra and Bubbles, swinging towards them with great power. Bubbles dodged one, dodged two, but the third clipped her tail which sent them spiralling down into the abyss.

When they stopped spiralling and had adjusted their bearings, the same great eye was once more staring at them, unblinking. Tetra turned to face the Kraken as four tentacles slowly came towards her from different directions.

"Give me back Tantalus!" Tetra yelled towards the great eye.

There was no response, only incoming tentacles surrounding all possible exits.

"You can keep the captain; I just want Tantalus!" she yelled towards the great eye once more.

A fifth tentacle come from above, grabbing both Tetra and Bubbles. Its grip was surprisingly gentle, but tight enough to hold them both without escape. They were dragged deeper into the abyss until they saw a giant beak below them.

Without a single second ticking by, barely even a few microseconds, they were thrown towards the beak. The beak opened and, the moment they were inside, it closed.

Down the dark abyss and into a new black hole.

Chapter 29
Inside the Kraken

At this point, Tetra was more fed up with being trapped inside large creatures than anything else in the whole world. True, on her island, she had felt trapped inside the classroom, but, at least she was safe, and safety had a certain appeal to it while trudging through the grease and grime of the insides of a large octopus.

It wasn't exactly dark but nor was it exactly light. There were glowing mushrooms dotted around, appearing to feed off the fleshy walls themselves. Whether the Kraken felt their presence was unknown, but trickles of green blood seemed to leak into the water, causing a misty, rancid atmosphere.

There was a small, steady slope in the distance. The murky water flowed in its direction and, much like a long corridor in a derelict temple, it was the only way to go. The Kraken's beak was firmly shut behind them and, without another thought, Tetra guided Bubbles slowly through the Kraken's passageway.

Further along, there were planks of wood drifting with the flow of the water. It wasn't just wood from Captain Neureus' ship, but wood from hundreds of others, from what appeared to be various points in time. Strange dinghies made from bamboo had been swallowed hole, with the skeletons of their sailors still sat inside them. It was a jungle: one which had been carved up and swallowed by a giant beast. Tetra found it ominous, to say the least, with perhaps the scariest part being the journey through time.

"This Kraken is a history book," she whispered to Bubbles, to which she responded with pockets of air dispersing from his nostrils.

"I wonder how long she has lived for," Tetra added, glancing around at wreckage after wreckage.

They soon arrived at what seemed to be a dead end. But, moments later, the flesh parted like a wave crashing against a rock, revealing a narrower, darker passage ahead. Once through the 'flesh door', it closed behind them with a disgusting, moist welp that made Tetra shudder.

The water was colder here. Not the icy cold from the northern waters, but the kind of cold that travels down a spine and makes it wince. A cold felt in an abandoned house rather than a refrigerator. A cold that consumes the inside rather than refreshes the outside. Chilling rather than frozen.

Everywhere should have been warm though. The inside of a Kraken should at least be lukewarm, if not, something above cold. But instead, the liquid surrounding them was much thicker than the sea and felt slightly greasy between her fingers.

She led Bubbles through the passage, with more wreckages rotting beneath the oily water. Small red orbs appeared, jittering past them like a school of small fish. One vanished inside the ribcage of a lonely skeleton that still clung to his knife and fork: a smashed plate not far from his resting place.

"The hungry became the dinner," smirked Tetra, causing Bubbles to give her a side eye. "You're right, I have been around Tantalus too long. I wonder where he is."

She turned away from the skeleton and looked around. There was nothing she hadn't already seen in the previous passage, nor was there likely to be anything if she went down another passage. Just corridors of wreckages and little else to rummage.

Two barrels were lined up next to each other, although one was tipped over. She gently rode Bubbles over and peered inside the upright barrel. It was half filled with a thick, black liquid that seemed to reflect her, at least a little. She could make out her hairline and her nose, but her eyes were vacant.

"Where's the turtle soup I was promised?" a voice yelled behind them.

Tetra turned Bubbles around sharply to find the skeleton was now awake and trying to lumber his broken body to his feet.

"I have no time for this," she said with a great sigh. She instructed Bubbles to ride towards the skeleton, and with a single clatter, a massive bump and an incredible smash, Bubbles rode straight through the skeleton. Afterwards, leaving nothing but a pile of bones.

"I remember you!" said the now skull without its body. "If ya find that turtle of yours, bring him this way, will ya? Imma bit 'ungry."

Tetra ignored him and carried on through the passage. Ahead, two shadows appeared, each belonging to a pair of new skeletons that had seemingly gone walking. They were dressed a little more like a pirate with one even having a customary eyepatch.

"Looky, Looky," one snarled towards Tetra. "It's dat wee gel from before." He nudged his companion, but a little too much, making his arm fall off. The arm began moving on its own, clawing its way towards Tetra and Bubbles.

"We orta tell Capin," said the armless companion.

"Nah, we be 'eroes," said the other pirate. "We take 'em back dead."

He drew his sword... or what he thought was a sword but which was more a fork, while his armless companion picked up a plank of wood. They walked menacingly towards Tetra and Bubbles.

"Don't let them close," said Tetra. "Show them what you've got."

Bubbles reared higher, reaching about a metre away from the ceiling. Then she pulled her neck back, took a deep gulp of water and spun around doing an underwater cartwheel. Then, not a moment too soon, she aimed a jet of bubbles straight at the pirates. Their skulls slumped from their necks. Then, their arms ripped from their shoulders, and their legs detached from their pelvises. Their ribs cracked and dissolved into the oily water.

"I told ya we shud of told Capin," said one of the skulls.

"Shut up, will ya?" said the other, before they descended into an argument that would probably last an eternity.

An eternity stuck inside a Kraken, unable to get away from each other... Tetra thought. *How fitting.*

The arm had other ideas though as it continued to crawl towards Tetra and Bubbles. It grabbed onto Bubbles' tail and gave it a huge squeeze. Bubbles whelped and started whizzing around uncontrollably.

Tetra was flung off Bubbles' back and bumped down on her behind on the ground that was covered in thick sludge that moved like a slug between her fingers. She screwed her nose up and mumbled in disgust. Then she looked up to see Bubbles still in a spot of bother.

"*Ha-ha-ha!* M' hand got the horsey," said one of the skulls.

Tetra shook her head. She rose, swam towards one of the pile of bones and grabbed one of the legs.

"Oi, oi, oi!" said the same skull. "That's m' leg."

Dragging the leg, she swam towards Bubbles, who was now frozen in exhaustion, panting uncontrollably. She raised the leg up like a baseball bat, took one good look at the hand, and smacked it with the leg. The hand and the leg both broke into several pieces, and some of it even into dust.

"Now look wot ya did!" said the skull.

"Shut up, will ya!" said the other. "Not like you can use dem anymore."

As they descended into bickering once more, Tetra knew she had to get out of there soon. Preferably with Tantalus. They carried on down the corridor where, to her disgust, the water became much more green and the odour much more rotten. Soon couldn't happen soon enough.

The corridor led to a large room, or what could be considered a room inside a Kraken. It was wider than the corridor, more spacious and had a higher ceiling. If she hadn't known better, she would have thought it just a spacious room. But this room was, she knew, within a Kraken.

And the walls moved though. Not like a fish or an eel, or even a crab. They contracted and squelched, and Tetra found it sickening. The walls of grey flesh were squeezing green ooze from its pores. It was no wonder there was a rotten stench.

There were crates around the edges and half a dinghy was tucked away in the corner. It was, though, what was happening in the middle of the room that was of greater concern.

A barrel, filled with the dark sludge, was on fire. Around the barrel stood five pirates, one of whom was Presumedly Roger. The other four were mere scalliwags, with barely enough legs between them. Indeed, one even looked like the leg he was using hadn't belonging to him in his previous life, and walked on it with a wobble.

Above the barrel was a cage hanging from the ceiling by a large steel chain. Inside the cage was a large turtle, hiding his face with his flippers and shuddering inside his shell.

"Tantalus!" Tetra called out. Immediately, the turtle's head popped out from behind his flippers and a smile beamed across his face.

That moment of happiness was short-lived though. While she had got Tantalus' attention, Tetra also managed to get the attention of Presumedly Roger and his four companions. They were now all glancing towards her, with menacing eyes and gritted teeth.

Chapter 30
Weird Reunions

In the distance behind them, Tetra could hear a strange dripping sound. Almost like soup desperately trying hard not to fall off a spoon. It did fall though, with a great drop into a puddle. The sound was dancing in the back of her ear like an annoying fly but, with Presumedly Roger slowly marching towards her, she put it to the back of her mind.

Presumedly Roger didn't look like any other pirate. He was an oddity, like a fire in the depths of the ocean, or a ship flying under the sea. Indeed, he summed up Tetra's strange adventure perfectly.

Unlike the other pirates, he was rather handsome, at least now he that had found his skeleton deep inside the Kraken. His teeth weren't missing, and were still pearly white. He wore clothes; denim jeans and a floral shirt, unlike a usual pirate. But here he was, in the depths of the sea, fighting with the pirates.

"It appears the girl has also been swallowed by the Kraken," said Presumedly Roger. "I imagine the captain would be delighted if we were to return her to him."

"Argh ya tawk like a weirdo," muttered one of the pirates.

"Excuse me?" asked Presumedly Roger.

"No mind, no mind, sir," the pirate muttered, edging away from Presumedly Roger.

The pirates began to advance on Tetra. The water inside the Kraken was thick with a musky green hue, making it difficult to move in. In fact, it was like crawling through custard, but less delicious.

"Oh, no, watch out, Tetwa," said Tantalus in the cage. "They think everything is jellyfwish."

"All right, Bubbles, just like before," she whispered in Bubbles' ear.

Bubbles began trotting forward at a steady pace. The seahorse seemed undeterred by Presumedly Roger's large scimitar and the other pirates' various ranges of cutlery and gardening utensils (although the rake could definitely do some damage).

Presumedly Roger lingered behind as the other four pirates began charging forwards. Soon, Bubbles' trot danced its way into a gallop, and when she galloped, she did so as hard as she could. But the water was too thick to reach the speed she would usually manage.

Bubbles stumbled through the first two pirates, smashing them into a pile of rubble, she knocked over the third removing his two legs, and missed the fourth who spun around from the sheer force of the charge, knocking his head off a barrel. Only Presumedly Roger was left in front, and when Bubbles came towards him, he dodged, and pushed out a leg, causing Tetra to go flying from Bubbles' back.

"You believe a calvary charge works inside a Kraken?" asked Presumedly Roger, polishing his scimitar with a small cloth. He came marching forward as Tetra stumbled up from the ground, her eyes fixed on his.

"Well, your friends are now a pile of bones," said Tetra.

"It does appear so, but they were never much more than a pile of bones in life either," he continued, stumbling forward with his scimitar raised. 'You shouldn't have come here. There are secrets here you are too fragile to understand."

"Fragile!" exclaimed Tetra, with the biggest of frowns on her face. She had now climbed back onto Bubbles' back and suddenly looked taller than she ever had before. Bubbles began trotting forward once more. "I've survived a hydra," she said as the trot became a little faster. "I've defeated a shark, been belched out a whale's tummy and now find myself inside a Kraken." Bubbles was galloping towards Presumedly Roger at great speed. "Fragile?" she repeated, as Bubbles rampaged into Presumedly Roger, knocking him onto the floor. His bones did not crumble though, nor did they become dislocated. A pile Presumedly Roger was not. He rose to his feet once more and smiled.

"Perhaps we can agree on delicate," he said, as he swung his scimitar towards Tetra. She dodged, and when he swung again, she dodged once more, before Bubbles swung her head towards the pirate, knocking him down once more.

"Ouch, ouch!" said a voice behind Tetra. She turned to see Tantalus blowing the flames that were licking at his flippers. "The fire is getting cwose," he cried.

"Tantalus, we're coming!" she cried, but before she could move, a great shadow rose over her. Presumedly Roger stood behind her, with his scimitar raised above his skull.

"Bye, poppit," he said. But before he could swing down, a strange orb came flying towards him, knocking him down once more.

Tetra gasped, turning around to see a bright orb, as white as the greatest of pearls, buzzing around Presumedly George like an enraged hornet.

"Pwease get me out!" cried Tantalus once more, as one flame started to engulf his flipper.

Tetra rode Bubbles at great speed, smashing into the cage and breaking it into several pieces and Tantalus swam out, away from the fire, sucking on his flipper.

"No more adventwures," he said. "Pwease no more."

Tetra gave him the biggest of hugs. He blushed and swung her around until reality set in for both of them.

"We gotta get out of here," said Tetra.

Presumedly Roger, who was presumedly having a bad time with the orb, had begun dashing down another corridor. The orb, seemingly chuffed with itself, buzzed around by the corridor's entrance.

"I guess the only way is the way Roger went," said Tetra. "Let's go."

"Ummm," said Tantalus, still sucking on his flipper. "There will pwobably be more piwates that way."

"Probably," said Tetra.

"Ummmm," Tantalus hummed once more. "We said no more adventwures."

Tetra turned to face Tantalus and held onto one of his flippers.

"After we get ourselves out of here, there will be no more adventures," she said, trying to believe it herself.

By now, the dripping sound was a constant reminder of where Tetra had been. It seemed to follow her, no matter where she went. Always behind, never anywhere else. The problem was it was now louder too, and it squelched like an elephant dancing in a bog.

Every now and then, she turned her head to look behind her. Nothing. Only crates and barrels, and wood that had not been a boat longer than it had been a boat. But the dripping remained. Relentlessly dripping.

The only thing now drowning out the sound of dripping was the sound of pirates cackling. And cackle they did. Even the captain was cackling, with perhaps even the loudest cackle of all. And when they turned a left corner, they found themselves standing in a large room; larger than the room before, with walls squelching with far greater thirst.

Before Tetra could step into the room, the strange orb came

whizzing up from behind, buzzing around her like a bee defending its nest. Unlike a bee, it pushed her back with a gentle poke, then resumed frantically buzzing around her face.

"Why did you do that for?" asked Tetra, trying to swim past it.

It was trying to talk but couldn't talk. It just whizzed around for around thirty seconds before appearing to sigh and look at the floor.

"What is it?" asked Tetra.

The orb tried to mimic something, but Tetra had no clue what, she just floated there with one eyebrow raised. The orb was just bobbing along from left to right, then right to left, before buzzing frantically once more.

"A jellyfwish?" blurted out Tantalus from nowhere, to which made the orb buzz even more frantically.

"Pirates? asked Tetra. "Yes, we know. We can hear them laughing. We will be fine."

She tapped on Bubbles' shoulder and he pushed past the orb. There in front of her was the ship once more, with around ten pirates carrying wood towards it. On the deck, the captain stood grinning over his minions, with a now worried-looking Presumedly Roger next to him.

Captain Neureus was grasping the harpoon with his left hand. It was shining a violent sort of light. A darkness flowed like flames and bounced off each wall like daggers slicing at leathery skin. Tetra could hear the harpoon through her veins once more. It appeared to be weeping.

"Ah, if it isn't my favourite adventurer!" said the captain, smiling towards Tetra. "I do like reunions, especially when they bring dinner. What do you think, Roger?"

"Oh, yes, Captain," said Presumedly Roger.

The other pirates were cackling until one pirate's arm fell off. They all turned towards him and laughed even more, to which he laughed too. They then faced back towards Tetra, waving their weapons in the water and began jeering obscenities at her.

"As you can see, my men have been reunited with their bodies… Or what's left of their bodies," said the captain. "Safe to say, the Kraken will regret consuming us. Her ink will be burnt and we will ride out of here on a wave of flames, isn't that right, Roger?"

"Yes, Captain," mumbled Presumedly Roger, under the raucous of cheers from the pirates below.

"Perhaps you should join us, Tetra?" said the captain. "I mean, you would have to ditch the donkey and the dinner, but what a small price to pay for freedom."

"Never!" snarled Tetra, her frown forcing her teeth to grit.

"I thought you might say that. Terribly unfortunate. Well, looks like girl is back on the menu, boys!"

Chapter 31
Dark Light

The pirates, or 'privateers' as Captain Neureus insisted on calling them, were marauding forwards towards Tetra, Tantalus and Bubbles. They had pieces of raw flesh dangling between what was left of their teeth and they ran like octopuses, but with four legs missing all on the same side.

Behind them on top of the ship stood Captain Neureus, holding the harpoon like a wizard's staff. The staff projected an intense dark light around the room, sinking to the ground when it hit a fleshy wall. Where it didn't sink, it cast shadows that echoed randomly across the space.

The pirate next to Captain Neureus – presumedly a man named Roger – appeared to be just a shadow of himself. His bony legs were shaking as he cast an eye towards Tetra and her friends. His skull, still handsome, had a crack beneath the right eye, in the shape of a tear.

With the pirates storming forward and the dripping sound behind, Tetra was beginning to feel claustrophobic. Something scared her about going backwards and going forwards now had its own problems. So she patiently waited while the pirates inched towards her.

The Kraken was stirring. There were small rumbles, and the fleshy walls were pulsing. The shaking ground had caused barrels of sludge to fall over, creating a sticky surface. For Tetra, Bubbles and

Tantalus, that was no problem: they could swim. For the skeletons, it was different.

A barrel of sludge had tipped over right in front of them, not only blocking their path, but sticking them to the ground. And a stuck pirate is an unhappy pirate. They began screaming obscenities and fighting amongst themselves.

"Well, that's unfortunate," sulked Captain Neureus. "Oh, well, come, Roger, let's get this ship moving."

The dripping behind now sounded like a waterfall of lava, falling into a pool from miles above. Tetra turned to see an oily figure moving slowly towards them. Strangely, the figure almost resembled Tetra, with the same wavy hair and the same frown on its forehead. The only difference was the vacant eyes... and the body made from sludge.

"Does this nightmare ever end?" asked Tetra, sighing in disbelief at what her eyes were witnessing.

The orb came racing into the room, nudging Tetra several times. It whizzed around her head and then moved in front of her and waited.

"You want us to follow you?" asked Tetra. The orb seemed to flicker and whizz around a little more before moving slightly further ahead than before.

"I don't see mwuch choice," said Tantalus, trying to keep a distance between him and the sludge beast.

Tetra nodded and they followed the orb towards the ship. Behind them, the sludge beast had now entered the room and was sliding its feet towards the stuck pirates. They stood still in silence, the only sound that could be heard was their bones creaking and their jaws dropping.

The captain himself had lost interest in Tetra and had turned towards the sludge beast. Even he, for all his quick-wittedness, seemed dumbstruck as the sludge beast approached his men. Roger had backed up behind him and was slowly edging further away.

The orb darted around the ship and towards a narrow entrance. Narrow was perhaps an understatement, at least for Tantalus. The fleshy walls had to stretch just for him, but with a little push, they soon opened.

They squeezed through the tight passage curved slightly right, then weaved slightly left. It smelled like a can of tuna, but was perhaps the nicest smell they had whiffed since being swallowed by the Kraken.

The passage was short, not much more than about ten widths of Tantalus', and ended in a small room containing nothing but a small boat, broken in half and sinking into the flesh of the Kraken.

"I know this boat," breathed Tetra, jumping off Bubbles' back and slowly swimming towards it. Then she collapsed to her knees by the boat and sunk her head towards the ground. The orb hovered above, as if it was watching her.

"This is my dad's boat!" she cried. "It has to be my dad's boat. It has the same scratch here." She pointed towards a small scratch on the outside of the boat. "It's from when I took the wheel one time and clipped a rock."

She made a half smile, the kind of smile that tries to wind its way to the cheeks but doesn't quite make it; the kind of smile that comes with a sigh at the end. She got up from her knees, floated towards the space between the two halves and peered in.

Inside there were several items she recognised. There was her dad's dagger, with the same leather strap around its handle. The fishnet was also definitely his, it had the scars where a hammerhead shark once got caught in it; that had been a scary day.

But there were some items she didn't recognise. Particularly, a book shoved underneath the seat. It was labelled, 'Roger's Diary'. She picked up and before she could start reading it, she noticed a bone peeking out from where the boat had cracked.

"Can you help me, Tantalus?" said Tetra. "I need to lift this boat up."

"Weave it to me," said Tantalus, flexing his flippers. He started pushing one half of the boat, but it wouldn't budge. He giggled then tried again. Nothing. He blew on his flippers, then tried once more. This time it moved without resistance, and before he could beam a smile, he noticed Bubbles had flipped it for him.

"Thanks, Bubbles," said Tetra. She looked at the ground to see bones, then fell to her knees once again.

"The shirt the skeleton wears," she cried. "That's my dad's, which means this has to be... my dad!"

Her tears rose from the sludgy water like dandelions in the wind. Each tear fluttered like a butterfly into the rancid water, sparkling into the darkness before fading like a shooting star. The orb stood still without a flicker or a jilt.

Both Bubbles and Tantalus embraced Tetra. She had never felt so powerless, so weak, but at the same time, she had never been so strong. As her tears faded into the grimace of the water, the orb slowly sunk towards the bones.

Soon, the orb was within the remains and one of the hands started twitching. Then the legs began kicking and the jaw began jittering.

Tetra looked up and saw the skeleton moving. She backed away, as did both Bubbles and Tantalus. They looked on as a skeleton rose to its feet and stared directly into Tetra's eyes.

"Dad?" she said, with tears rolling down her cheeks.

"That's correct," said a voice from behind them. Tetra turned to see Presumedly Roger staring back at them. He walked with his scimitar pointing forwards. "And this is his fault, everything."

"Still blaming me, aye, Roger?" said a voice by the broken boat. Tetra turned to see the skeleton holding her dad's dagger and walking forward.

"I'm so sorry, Tetra," the skeleton said while walking towards her. "I didn't mean to leave you all those years ago. I was on my way home when I was led astray and taken by a giant beast."

"They were your directions, Jean," said Presumedly Roger. "You landed us here."

"I made mistakes," said Jean. "But I tried to get us out of here, I tried to get us home. You left me here for dead."

"You were already dead, Jean," argued Presumedly Roger. "We both are. Look at you. You're a skeleton just like me."

Presumedly Roger walked past Jean and towards the boat, still pointing his scimitar in the direction of Tetra's dad. He gently leaned downwards, grabbed his diary and walked towards the exit.

"It's time for me to get out of this Kraken once and for all," said Presumedly Roger. "And only the captain can make that happen." Before Jean, whose fists were clenched like lobster claws, could react, Roger left back down the narrow passage.

"Who is he, Dad?" asked Tetra.

"It doesn't matter." Jean smiled, and knelt towards her. Then they hugged... as well as Tetra could hug a skeleton anyway. And though his bones creaked and she was sure she might have accidentally broke one of his ribs, but he seemed unfazed.

"Roger is right though," said Jean. "It's time to find a way out of here."

They left the room down the narrow passage and entered back into the large room, where the captain's ship lay. But it was now dark. Not the darkness that comes from the absence of light, but the kind of darkness that only the antagonist of light can achieve.

The dark light sunk to the floor like a rock in a river and rolled around like a small tornado trying to lift a whale. It was smothering the floor around the ship, trying to climb onto its deck. On top of the deck stood the captain, with the harpoon raised high, leaking dark light around the room.

In the distance, the sludge beast was crawling towards them.

Chapter 32
The Sludge Reflection

The ship appeared to be moving, about as fast as a conch shell but, nonetheless, it was moving towards the exit. The captain himself must have known it was moving as he was standing by the wheel cackling to himself. As for Presumedly Roger, he was presumedly on the ship too.

The sludge beast was edging closer to Tetra. It was like a dark mirror, reflecting Tetra but giving her image a menacing look, as if Tetra had jumped into sewage and began rolling around.

Suddenly, Bubbles came charging forward, Tetra jumped onto her back, then the seahorse trotted around, circling the sludge beast, keeping both eyes on the grimacing shadow before them. Tetra had no weapon to wield, not even a stick or a spoon. She put on a brave face but felt ultimately out of her depth once more.

"*Hahaha!*" came a chuckle from the ship. "It appears your hourglass has run out of sand."

"There's plenty left yet," Tetra said through gritted teeth.

"On the contrary, my favourite adventurer. This is one adventure too far for a little girl."

"Don't listen to Neureus," came a voice she recognised. "I still believe death hasn't met me even though I'm nothing but bones now. I'm getting you out of here."

Tetra's father, Jean, came stumbling forward, waving his knife towards the sludge beast. The sludge beast turned to face him, and before he could swipe his knife, it shot a stream of sludge at him, pushing him back against the flesh wall.

"Dad!" cried Tetra, before her eyes narrowed towards the sludge beast. "Give it all you've got, Bubbles."

The sludge beast turned to face Tetra once more, suddenly standing a lot taller. Sludge began to foam beneath it as it rose higher and higher. The foam created a sludge tail, and then sludge fins and a sludge snout. It had become a terrible sludge Bubbles with a sludge Tetra on top.

Bubbles slowed and came to a halt about a metre from the sludge beast. Tetra then guided her around it, and they began circling once again.

"*Bahaha!*" came the cackle once more. "Take a look at them, Roger, stuck in the mud."

"Yes, Captain," said Presumedly Roger.

"Well, as they say in some faraway land. *Au Revoir!*" The captain's ship was now at the edge of the corridor and slowly moving out of sight. Tetra wasn't concerned with him at this point though. Where he was heading, she didn't care. She had her own problems.

Bubbles blew a huge stream of bubbles towards the sludge, but they were mostly absorbed into the muck of the body. The sludge beast barely stirred. Not even a wince. It remained still staring into Tetra's eyes.

"I think we should just wun," said Tantalus, trying to help put Jean's leg back together.

"No use, there's more sludge where that came from," said Jean.

Tetra picked up a long piece of wood from one of the broke crates. It wasn't much of a spear. In fact, it wasn't much of a stick at all. But she felt she needed something defeat the sludge beast, something more than she already had.

"OK, Bubbles," said Tetra, stroking the seahorse's neck. "This needs to be your biggest charge yet."

The seahorse snorted bubbles into the thick bog that had grown around them, and began trotting towards the sludge beast. The sludge beast also snorted bubbles in the thick bog, and then within a few seconds, grew its own sludge weapon. Tetra realised it was mimicking everything Tetra and Bubbles did.

Like medieval knights jousting, they charged at each other with their weapons drawn. And when they struck, there could only be one winner. Tetra fell from Bubbles and was thrown into a pile of crates, her weapon snapped in half.

The sludge beast turned to face her once more, seated silently on its sludge seahorse, still wielding its sludge weapon. Its body was dripping more sludge than before, each drip turning the water even more sour.

Tetra picked up another weapon, this one a piece of wood from the one of the crates she had just been thrown into. It was sharper than the other piece and slightly thicker. She felt more confident with this lance.

"We go again, Bubbles," she said as Bubbles swept her back onto her back.

"That won't work, Tetra," said her father, now with most of his bones back into place. "The sludge beast is like a mirror. It'll copy everything you do and always come out stronger."

"Well, we have to try something," Tetra replied, riding Bubbles into position. "One more time Bubbles. This time we will win."

Jean slapped his bony hand across his face and continued watching as Tantalus pushed his last bone into place, when it had clicked in, he rose to his feet once more.

Once again, Tetra and the sludge beast jostled for victory. Tetra charged once more, Bubbles pounding her tail against the water. The sludge beast matched their pace, and when Tetra raised her weapon, the sludge beast raised its own.

As their bodies crossed paths, Tetra stuck her weapon into the sludge of the beast. She grasped on tight, then she was flung off Bubbles and whirled around like a ragdoll. Then, just as Tetra thought the sludge beast was done, it flung her across the room and into some barrels. Her piece of wood still stuck in the beast's sludge body.

"The sludge," said her dad from across the room. "The sludge is flammable!"

Tetra stared at her hands to see that sludge had leaked all over them. It wasn't from the sludge beast but from the barrels she had tumbled into. One had tipped over and the sludge was flowing towards the beast.

The beast had now lost its sludge seahorse and was marauding towards her, still wielding its sludge weapon.

"Quick, Tantalus, distract it!" yelled Tetra across the room.

"Ummm, deeerrrr, ummmm…" jittered Tantalus with his flippers covering his mouth.

"Quick!" yelled Tetra once more, as she rubbed two pieces of wood together. The sludge beast moved deceptively slow, like a snail that makes it to the end of the garden while no one is looking.

"Ummm, deerrr, ummmm… oooo?"

Tantalus' head turned to Jean, who was looking back at him like a wounded soldier.

"Don't even think about it," said Jean. "I've only just been put back together."

"'Sorry, sorry, Tetwa's papa. Too wate to think," jittered Tantalus, as he pulled one of Jean's arms off with his beak and launched it at the sludge beast.

The sludge beast turned to face Tantalus and Tetra's father. Jean's arm was wedged in the body of the sludge beast and this seemed to be causing it annoyance. Its body began rumbling, and when it rumbled, the sludge tumbled, and when it tumbled, the sludge began fumbling. Then, without a moment too soon, Jean's arm burst from the sludge beast and onto the wall just above Tantalus' head.

Tantalus gulped as the sludge beast began moving slowly towards him. But just then, a spark fizzed across Tetra's pieces of wood, and then another small jolt of fire sizzled onto the oil leaking from the barrels.

Fire brewed and then stampeded across the sludge like an anchovy feeding frenzy. It raged through the paths the sludge filled and tumbled into each corner of the room. Tantalus and Jean sat hugging each other as the sludge beast, marauding towards them, was set alight.

Loud screeches rumbled from the sludge beast as it sunk to its knees in a rage of flames. The screeches whirled through Tetra's ears and she sunk to her knees with her hands pressed against her ears to block the sound.

The walls squelched and the floor shook. And, as the flames engulfed the ceiling, the sludge beast melted to the floor. And when the screeching stopped, the sludge beast was gone, leaving nothing but ash and soot drifting in the murky water.

Tetra rose up and sighed, before swimming towards Bubbles and stroking her chin.

The Kraken had stirred once more. The fire was climbing the walls and scorching the ceiling; walls and the ceiling which were, of course, the insides of the Kraken. Its flesh dripped green pus as the temperature had risen to above bearable. As the rumbles raged, a strange sense of dread crept through Tetra's veins. As she stared into the corridor, her eyes widened. It was just like it had been on that fateful day, when she had been swept away from her island.

A large wave of sludge was rolling though the corridor towards them.

Chapter 33
Sludge Tsunami

The belly of the sea is insatiable. It's always hungry. Always looking to swallow more. On that fateful day when the tsunami swept Tetra away, she had been merely a snack in the never-ending hunger of the sea.

And now it had come back for more.

The huge tsunami of sludge was fast approaching. On top of the wave, the captain's ship was being towed back into the large room.

"*Argh,* I've had enough of this beast," came a shout from atop the ship.

"There's fire behind us, Captain," came another voice.

"Of course, there is, there's always something new with this beast."

"What should I do, Captain?"

"Release the anchor."

"Yes, Captain."

As the ship was helped into the room by the kindness of the wave, an anchor was dropped down into the flesh of the beast, causing green liquid to ooze once more into the water. The sludge wave cast a shadow over the entire room, and Tetra's eyes widened as memories of that fateful day tormented her mind.

"Quick!" came a muffled voice bouncing between the bones in her eyes. "Quick, Tetra, over here!"

She turned to see her father, on the back of a turtle, trying to usher her somewhere hazy. She looked back towards the sludge wave to see its body hanging above her and the ship almost on top of her. Then a large seahorse charged towards her and carried her away from the wave.

It was mostly a blur, but maybe that was better, because the tsunami before had been anything but a blur. But as Tetra whizzed just above the sludge, the confusion of the captain's ship became clearer, and when the sludge wave crashed against the wall, the angry voice of the captain echoed into her veins.

And when she landed, she did so on the captain's ship. She stood up to see the captain glaring at her from the wheel, and a man, Presumedly Roger, standing just behind him.

"If you want to get out of here, we're going to have to work together again, Roger," said a voice next to her. She turned to see it was her father.

"Work together?" cackled the captain. "This lad wants to work with you, Roger." He nudged Presumedly Roger in the ribs and then looked back at Jean. "Whatcha gonna do? Use the turtle's shell as a lifeboat?"

A loud shriek came from within the Kraken, and the walls began to shake and rumble. The room was now filling up with sludge, and it was soon set alight, becoming a sea of fire.

Presumedly Roger was jittering behind the captain. He was gulping more than a goldfish and kept glancing at the fiery sea behind him. The captain, though, seemed unfazed.

"The Kraken won't be able to hold its food down too long," snarled the captain. "It already appears to have a little indigestion."

Tetra glanced over the side of the ship to see the anchor digging deep into the Kraken. The green liquid oozed into the flames, creating purple sparks all over the surface of the sludge. As the room filled with sludge, the ship began to move, dragging the anchor across the Kraken's flesh, making the Kraken shriek once more.

Only, this time, the shriek lasted longer. And as she shrieked, the room filled with more and more sludge, which piled into the flames. Then, with a snap from the anchor and a gulp from the Kraken, the fiery sludge flowed out of the room, taking the ship and everyone on it with it.

It rushed through the large corridor, past the fleshy door and out of the Kraken's mouth in a vomit of fire. As the flames cooled in the darkness of the sea, Tetra looked up to see a huge eye staring back at her. Then, the Kraken began pushing her tentacles downwards.

Underneath the Kraken was hidden a vast wooden plug. It was so vast that only the Kraken was bigger than it. And when she pushed her massive tentacles against it, the plug resisted. But then, gradually, it loosened, and then, to Tetra's surprise, the plug popped out, letting all the water in the world to come rushing out, and carrying the ship with it.

Tetra looked back towards the Kraken. There was an endless waterfall pouring down into the darkness. There were stars all around her, and some clusters even looked like faraway galaxies. But what shocked her the most was the place where she had been.

"I was in a glass bottle the whole time," she stuttered to herself.

It was massive, like its own galaxy, but not exactly. More like a universe within a universe, akin to Russian dolls in space.

Through the glass she could see places where she had been; such as the forest and the white walls of the coral reef, to the desolate grasslands and the icy kingdom. Around each place, the water level was decreasing fast.

Below her was mere darkness. Even the light from the stars couldn't escape it. They just swirled into the oblivion that was edging closer and closer towards them.

"Sorry, no free passage," came the captain's voice behind her, as he marauded towards her, swinging the harpoon.

Tetra ducked just in time, landing on her knees, then struggling to get back up. The captain took another swipe before Tantalus came bundling into him, pushing him back across the deck.

When Tetra finally got to her feet, she saw her dad and Presumedly Roger fighting on the deck above. Their knives were clashing and their swings were heavy, their bones crumbling to powder each time they were hit.

She then looked back at the captain who had also now got back to his feet and was staring back at her. The dark light from the harpoon rose into the stars above, antagonising the light as it flowed in all directions.

Bubbles wasn't as agile without the ocean around her and she bounced around trying to charge towards the captain. Tetra stroked her neck and smiled at her. "This is my fight," she said before turning back to the captain.

"Captain Nereus!" she called.

"It seems the girl has found her voice," chuckled the captain, whose harpoon was now shaking with an erratic force.

"The harpoon," said Tetra with a momentary pause. "I don't think you can control its power."

The captain laughed, but then he bellowed. His eyes turned on Tetra, seeming to zoom in, causing the hair on her arms to stand on end. She took a step back as the dark light from the harpoon grew more intense.

"No, your ride ends here," the captain snarled, pointing the harpoon at Tetra. Dark light frothed like a wave, crashing into the sand, then dripped around the edge of the harpoon like a hurricane tumbling onto an island.

The sea falling from the bottle had turned dark and fell slowly like sludge. The jelly beasts appeared, drifting in the galactic sky like plastic bags in the wind. The dark light from the harpoon hit them and they fluttered down into the sludge, littering the surface with their gigantic bodies.

One of the Kraken's tentacles appeared out of the bottle, swirling its way towards the captain, but to no avail, but the dark light hit it and it recoiled back into the bottle with a screech. The light from the stars was scared away and replaced with balls of intense dark light, that seemed to sizzle in their own darkness.

The captain's eyes turned purple, his bony hands were cracking and his ribs looked brittle. His teeth started chattering, and then grinding until two teeth snapped out of his mouth. The river of dark light flowed around him until it formed a whirlpool. He was drenched in the dark light with only the harpoon sticking out from its shell.

"This is bad," gulped Tantalus. "This is really bwaaaad." He covered his eyes with his flippers and continued to mumble to himself.

"I can hear the harpoon," Tetra whispered. "It's scared."

She began walking closer towards the captain, who remained veiled in the dark light. She was cautious, secretly afraid, but nonetheless determined to get closer to the harpoon. Soon, she was so close that the dark light made her hands feel damp.

She peered through the dark light and saw a glimpse of the captain. He was standing motionless, and as stiff as a skeleton should be. His head had rolled back but purple still gleamed from the holes in his skull.

Tetra edged her hand forward and slowly touched the harpoon. It pushed her back with a snarling whimper. Sludge dripped from her hand and scurried across the deck of the ship. She reached her hand out again and this time grasped the harpoon as hard as she could.

This time, the harpoon wheezed through her veins. Her eyes turned purple, and her head tilted back just like the captain's had.

But it was only brief.

Her head tilted forwards once more. Purple turned to gold. And the sludge began to turn into a crisp, summer's light. The dark light began to recede, and the stars returned to the skies. And there were many skies. Every galaxy in the distance seemed to have new skies as the golden light broke through the wall of dark light.

The captain sunk to his knees. And as life returned to his fragile body, he looked up at the now golden figure of Tetra.

Chapter 34
The Final Wave Home

Tetra felt something she had never felt before when she looked into the captain's eyes. It was an aching feeling that stabbed into her chest like the harpoon had into the great whale. She was sure it wasn't sympathy, as the captain had done this to himself. Nor was it anger, for the golden light couldn't shine with the feelings of anger.

She thought it must be pity.

Yes, that was it, she pitied him.

His tyranny over the sea had ended and he was fast becoming nothing more than an empty shell. His had lost his strength and now he could only kneel before Tetra. His stern eyes had become nothing more than holes filled with sorrow, and the cracks in his skull widened into canyons.

But the effect on Tetra was quite the opposite. She glowed like a nebula shouting into the darkness. She stood differently. No longer did the tide pull her, but she pulled it. The golden light around her moved like gentle waves, tumbling like candy floss in a gentle breeze.

The sea pouring from the bottle was no longer sludge, but crisp, clean water that reflected the galaxies above. The jelly beasts rose once more, free from the sludge on their tentacles, and rode the waves behind the ship.

The Kraken, no longer tamed by the dark light, appeared; its tentacles emerging from the bottle one by one.

Behind the Kraken's tentacles, something else was emerging, something different.

The captain slowly turned his head towards the bottle. It was now distant, but still covered most of the sky in the horizon. On the deck above, both Jean and Presumedly Roger had stopped fighting. They were both looking towards the bottle.

A beast emerged with four sunken necks. The fifth neck, though, rose above the stars and had a ferocious set of teeth, crimson liquid dripping from each blade. It was as if a fish had morphed into a dragon, or a dragon had tumbled into the sea and became a little fish.

It was the Hydra, or at least what was left it. A Hydra without its other heads. A Hydra without its siblings. A Hydra with menace in its eyes.

"The one that got away," muttered the captain, his eyes tiptoeing back into his skull.

Tetra stood over the captain like a lighthouse in a hurricane. The harpoon shone light around the galactic skies, that ricocheted between the stars.

The Hydra roared like thunder and came down like lightning. Its large jaw tumbled down like waves falling off the edge of the world. And when the wave hit the captain, it did so with the force of a thousand teeth, snatching him up like a tornado.

The Hydra carried the captain back towards the bottle. The tide of the water falling from the universe was not strong enough to hold back the raw power of an angry Hydra. The bottle was nearly empty, but the storm had only just begun.

All the while, the Kraken still waved her tentacles around. They moved like eels towards the ship. Jean and Presumedly Roger watched on as two tentacles approached them.

One coiled around Presumedly Roger and lifted him off the ship. It squeezed so tight he couldn't move or squeak and his bones could be hard crackling gently like corn popping in a pan.

The other came for Jean who swung his knife at it. It curled away briefly, before returning with more power and more confidence. It grabbed Jean and began to carry him towards the bottle.

"Dad!" yelled Tetra towards him but, just like Presumedly Roger, he was unable to move or call out. "Bubbles, quick!"

Bubbles tumbled towards Tetra, flung her on her back and jumped into the falling water.

"This is a bwad idea," said Tantalus, as he slumped his way to the upper deck to peer over the side.

The power of the flowing water was strong; the force of gravity into the darkness created the most turbulent current yet. Bubbles struggled and had started going backwards before she had really started going forwards.

"This is your moment," whispered Tetra in Bubbles' ear. "There's not a horse I'd have more faith in to push through this tide and save my dad."

Bubbles roared once more, and her eyes became more intense. She stopped going backwards but still wasn't really going forwards.

"You can do this," said Tetra, with a little more assertion. "I know you can do this."

The harpoon's gold light grew and, as it grew, it enveloped over Bubbles. No longer was she just another seahorse, but her skin was tickled with golden light through each one of her scales.

She roared once more and it echoed towards every star in the sky, and probably even made it to every galaxy. The water seemed to stop falling, or at least it looked so, as Bubbles ploughed through it like Tantalus through a flock of jellyfish.

Bubbles galloped with the power of a hundred horses and Tetra raised her harpoon towards the Kraken's tentacle as they charged forwards together.

Then the harpoon appeared to grow longer, becoming much more like a paladin's pike rather than a fisherman's spear. They light trickled over the universe and a puddle became an ocean. The Kraken's tentacles were recoiling quick and fast approaching the neck of the bottle.

"One last push!" said Tetra, stroking Bubble's neck with her right hand as her left hand held the harpoon straight.

Bubbles pushed through the water and the waves around her crashed behind her. She travelled so fast that there could have been tsunamis behind her. But it didn't matter, all that mattered was what was in front of them.

The Kraken's tentacles had almost retracted in. Jean looked almost broken in the clutches of its grasp. There was crackling as the Kraken coiled tighter like an anaconda squeezing its prey.

Bubbles glided close to the tentacle and as she brushed past the gigantic arm of the Kraken, the golden harpoon slashed across its thick skin. A screech from within the bottle roared and large cracks in the bottle appeared above the lagoon.

The Kraken let go of Jean who fell on the back of Bubbles, just behind Tetra. Bubbles leapt and they landed back on the ship to a welcoming Tantalus, who remained as confused as he always seemed to be.

Back at the bottle, the other tentacle recoiled back inside the neck, and Presumedly Roger disappeared with it. Only the jelly beasts continued to fall with the water as the last drop rolled out of the bottle. And now there was darkness below: so much darkness that not even the light from the harpoon could escape it.

When the last drop from the bottle fell, the cork rolled back into place. Then, in a sudden jolt, the cracks that had begun rampaging across the bottle stopped. And when they stopped, the bottle exploded. Trillions of shards of glass littered across the universal sky and the force pushed the ship faster towards the darkness.

"Hold on tight," yelled Jean, as he pulled himself up from the deck, with less ribs than he had hands. "We've got to guide this ship down steady."

The closer to the darkness they were, the more notorious the atmosphere became. It was like a storm, but instead of rain there was light, and instead of their clouds there was empty pockets of intense darkness.

Tantalus was sliding around the deck on his belly, and if turtles could vomit, he sure looked like he would have done already. Bubbles had her tail wrapped around one of the masts, from which the captain's flag had already blown off and pulled in by the darkness. Tetra held onto the back of Bubbles, and the harpoon held onto her.

Jean's legs were now off the ground as his hands tried to control the wheel. The sails, still stained with the crimson mist, fluttered like a pufferfish ready to explode. And the light from the harpoon spun around until it was split into pieces by the darkness.

"I did say no more adwentures," Tantalus could be heard mumbling, as he continued to spin around the deck.

"This is the last, Tantalus, this is the last," said Tetra, just as she was flung from Bubbles' back, landing with one hand still on the mast and the harpoon pointed towards the darkness.

"Tetra!" her father shouted. "Hold on!"

But it was difficult to hold on. The darkness was too powerful. Her smallest finger slipped from her grip. Then the largest finger slipped from her grip. Then all her fingers slipped and she flew from the ship and towards the darkness.

"Tetra!" She could hear her dad's voice yelling, as she tumbled towards the darkness.

And towards the darkness she went.

She saw all the darkness as it rolled between the golden light of the harpoon. She twisted her body to face the darkness as the golden light whirled towards it. She closed her eyes and pointed the harpoon in front of her.

And then, Tetra woke up somewhere else.

Chapter 35
The Tide Over the Horizon

Tetra felt different.

Sand whispered through her fingers. It was subtle, like a small fish tickling through the leaves of a kelp tree, but she knew it was sand.

But it was different sand.

It didn't feel damp, or even cold, but it was warm and dry. Almost brittle. And there was a touch of wood beneath it.

Even the water felt different. It didn't flow with the same power and didn't seem to drag her along. Indeed, she stayed in the same place, lying on the sand, as it pushed itself against her body. If she could describe the water with one word, she would describe it as air.

When she opened her eyes, she had to immediately close them once more. The sun was bright, brighter than it usually was. It also felt much more intense on her skin, and the heat was inescapable.

She opened her eyes once more and tried to swim to an upright position. The water didn't carry her though. The more she moved her arms, the more ridiculous she felt.

This can't be water, thought Tetra, with a small frown creating tiny ditches on her forehead. She moved her head to the side and saw a thin layer of sand blanketing a wooden platform. She then looked to the other side and saw the same wooden platform with a duvet of sand.

This isn't the sea, she thought once more, as the tiny ditches on her forehead smoothed away. *I'm out of the sea.* She sat up to look around and catch her bearings, or to make sure her bearings didn't catch her.

"This looks like home." She smiled. "This must be home. This is the dock where I... I was swept away." She stood up and looked towards the horizon. There was a ship approaching on the horizon, but she couldn't see it properly.

She started walking across the dock platform. On the beach to her right, a small recently hatched turtle was struggling to make its way to the sea. Seagull flocks were flying above with their eyes looking directly at the hatchling.

Tetra, though, had other plans.

She walked off the wooden platform and gently swept the small turtle into her hands. She then carried it to the sea and let a tiny wave carry it into the sea. The turtle looked back at her, appeared to wink and then swam away.

"I sure miss Tantalus," said Tetra as she watched the turtle swim away. "I hope he's all right. I hope Bubbles is too, and of course, Dad."

The ship that was on the horizon was now a little closer. Tetra could make out some pink-looking sails and a rather worse-for-wear looking hull. Nonetheless, it was still afloat and heading towards the dock. She headed back onto the wooden platform and walked towards the edge of the dock.

She peered over the edge and saw small fish scattering around the stilts. There was lots of seaweed curling around each stilt and growing up towards the dock. There were also small movements inside the seaweed, that it didn't seem to be caused by the current.

She knelt and looked closer. It definitely wasn't the current. There was a small tail inside the seaweed moving agitatedly. Tetra gently grasped the seaweed and turned a leaf over. Underneath, there was a small seahorse tangled in the weed. It was, fortunately, an easy knot to untie, and within seconds Tetra had set the little seahorse free.

The seahorse turned around, appeared to blow bubbles into the sea and swam away towards the ship.

"That was just like Bubbles," said Tetra. "I miss her."

The ship was now fast approaching the dock. It was a ship Tetra recognised, although not from the island itself. The crimson sails, the tattered and slightly burnt hull, the gnawed wheel. It could only be Captain Neureus' ship.

But, when it came closer, Tetra could clearly see that the man behind the wheel wasn't Captain Neureus.

Nor was it a skeleton of any sorts.

She knew the face from many years ago. A familiar face that she had missed.

It was her father. Jean. A man that was not a skeleton any more but fully fleshed. He waved at her, and with a smile stretching from cheek to cheek, Tetra waved back.

Swimming around the ship was a tiny turtle, appearing to be eating something. Tetra didn't quite know, but it was definitely munching its way into a belly full of pain. And a small seahorse that kept blowing bubbles into the air.

Tetra smiled. She was home.

The End